THE DRAGON'S QUEEN

DRAGON LORDS: A QURILIXEN WORLD NOVEL

MICHELLE M. PILLOW

MICHELLE M. PILLOW® - MICHELLEPILLOW.COM

ABOUT THE DRAGON'S QUEEN

DRAGON LORDS 9

Dragon-shifter Romance

by Michelle M. Pillow

A Prequel Story

Mede of the Draig knows three things for a fact: As the only female dragon-shifter of her people, she is special. She can kick the backside of any man. And she absolutely doesn't want to marry.

Mede has spent a lifetime trying to prove she's as strong as any male warrior. Unfortunately, being the special, rare creature she is, she's been claimed as the future bride to nearly three dozen Draig—each one confident that when they come for her hand in marriage, fate will choose them. When the men aren't bragging about how they're going to marry her, they're acting like she's a delicate rare flower in need of their protection.

But Mede is far from a shrinking solarflower.

Prince Llyr of the Draig knows four things for a fact: He is the future king of the dragon-shifters. He must act honorably in all ways. He absolutely, positively is meant to marry Lady Mede. And she is dead set against marriage.

Llyr's fate rests in the hands of a woman determined not to have any man. With a new threat emerging amongst their cat-shifting neighbors, a threat whose eyes are focused firmly on Mede, time may be running out. It is up to him to convince her to be his dragon queen.

Dragon Lords books 1-8 follow a concurrent time line. The fun of this is that the events you read in one book might be examined from a different point of view, sometimes with overlapping or expanded scenes, sometimes with events you might have wondered about in another book. You might even discover secrets as characters interact with each other. I recommend reading them in order to get the full effect. However if you bought the books out of order, no worries, each book is technically a standalone story for the hero and heroine.

Dragon Lords Books 1 - 4

The dragon-shifting princes have no problem with commitment. In one night, they will meet and choose their life mate in a simplistic ceremony involving the removing of masks and the crushing of crystals. With very few words spoken and the shortest, most bizarre courtship in history, they will bond to their women forever. And once bonded, these men don't let go...

Too bad nobody explained this to their brides.

Dragon Lords Books 5-8

The noblemen brothers aren't new to the sacred Qurilixian bridal ceremony. After several failed attempts at finding a bride, it's hard to get excited about yet another festival. No matter how honorably they try to live, it would seem fate thinks them unworthy of such happiness—that is until now.

With very few words spoken and the shortest, most bizarre courtship in history, they will bond to their women forever. And once bonded, these men don't let go...

Too bad nobody explained this to their brides.

Dragon Lords Book 9

Before four princes and four noblemen found their brides, before the death of the Var King Attor and the threat of the Tyoe miners, there was a time of peace on the planet of Qurilixen. It was not a strong peace, but it had lasted for quite some time between the cat-shifting Var kingdom and their northern neighbors the dragon-shifting Draig. It lasted because both sides had very little to do with each other.

This was the time before the great war came to rift the planet apart—dragon against cat. The only battles were skirmishes along the borderlands over territory and drunken brawls that erupted to prove which shifter side was of superior strength. It is here the dragons found their queen.

Spin-off Series

Dragon Lords is the first installment in the multiple bestselling romance series. As of this publication, there are nine Dragon Lords books.

The series continues with the *Lords of the Var®* series, Space Lords series, Dynasty Lords Series, Captured by a Dragon-Shifter series, Galaxy Alien Mail Order Brides series, and Qurilixen Lords series.

There will be more books and more series to come. They can be read alone, but the author recommends reading books in order of release.

For details please visit www.michellepillow.com

Dragon Lords Series
Barbarian Prince
Perfect Prince
Dark Prince
Warrior Prince
His Highness The Duke
The Stubborn Lord
The Reluctant Lord
The Impatient Lord
The Dragon's Queen

***Lords of the Var*® Series**
The Savage King

The Playful Prince
The Bound Prince
The Rogue Prince
The Pirate Prince

Captured by a Dragon-Shifter Series
Determined Prince
Rebellious Prince
Stranded with the Cajun
Hunted by the Dragon
Mischievous Prince
Headstrong Prince

Space Lords Series
His Frost Maiden
His Fire Maiden
His Metal Maiden
His Earth Maiden
His Woodland Maiden

Dynasty Lords Series

Seduction of the Phoenix

Temptation of the Butterfly

To learn more about the Qurilixen World series of
books and to stay up to date on the latest book list
visit www.MichellePillow.com

To Bella Monster because she thinks she's a dragon. She also thinks she's the boss of me. She's not. I'm the boss of her. Hold on, she's hungry, I need to go get her a treat.
To Lord Winston the official man of the house who whines like we're neglecting him. I see his point. He should be petted at every possible second of the day.
To the army of cats amassing outside. We surrender.
To Lady Annabelle for keeping Winston in check.
To Fiona, beanies.
To B.
<3

CHAPTER 1

PROLOGUE

DRAIG NORTHERN MOUNTAINS, Planet of Qurilixen

There were three things Medellyn knew for a fact. She was special. She could kick the ass of any boy. And she did not want to marry and have babies.

She was special.

Medellyn was one of the only dragon-shifting females in all the universe, and definitely in all of the Draig population. Only once in a thousand births, was a female dragon-shifter born. She was rare, or so everyone kept telling her. Her childhood was a strange contradiction. Her very proper mother tried to treat her as if she were some sacred crystal that might crack. Her warrior father tried to make her train like a boy while dressing like a girl.

She could kick the ass of any boy.

Medellyn hated when males tried to act as if she were weak and needed protection. Her dragon was just as fierce as any of theirs, probably more so. To prove her point, she'd gladly pummel any who had challenged her to the ground…and some who hadn't.

She *absolutely, positively* did not want to marry and have babies.

Being the special, rare creature she was, in the twenty not-so-sweet girlhood years of her life she'd been claimed as the future bride of nearly three dozen boys—each one confident that when they came of the age to marry, she would make their crystals glow and they hers.

Glowing crystals wasn't just a metaphor. On the day she was born, her father journeyed to Crystal Lake like all the new fathers did. He dove beneath the waves, swam down to the deepest part and pulled her stone from the lakebed. Like all Draig children, she wore the stone around her neck, and would continue to wear it until the day it glowed, telling her which of the dragon-shifting men she was destined by the gods to marry. From that moment on their souls would join, they'd hear each other's thoughts, they'd have dragon babies, whatever. Technically she might be destined to marry an offworlder like most Draig men, but no one on her planet seemed to think so.

Gods' bones, she hoped she wasn't destined to end up with any of the idiots on her planet. They had yet to impress her.

When it was her turn to go to the Breeding Festival, the crystal would glow, signifying her *curse* for all to see. Well, her *blessing* as her mother called it. Lady Grace did not appreciate her daughter calling marriage a curse. Grace did not appreciate a lot of things that Medellyn liked, such as swords and bows, ceffyl riding, camping alone in the forest, hunting, sparring, smashing arrogant looks off of dragon men's faces.

It was a fight with her mother that had sent her running through the mountain forest. Medellyn hated the woman, hated what her mother wanted her daughter to be. Grace was only a human, brought to their planet as a bartered bride. She'd married Medellyn's father without question and spent most of her days completely in docile agreement with whatever her husband said. Medellyn couldn't imagine taking anyone else's opinions over her own.

Her father, Axell, was a highly praised warrior in the Draig army and carried the title of Top Breeder of the ceffyls. The man's whole life focused on four things: his wife, his only child, and mares and steeds. Her father was a very important man, but his work kept him away from home several nights a week as he slept outdoors with the herd. With a three-year gestation period and only about a fifty percent live birth rate, the animals were not a resource that could be easily renewed. His ceffyls supplied the soldiers with mounts and farmers used them for beasts of burden to help with the fields.

Like Axell, Medellyn was a proud dragon. Had she been born male, she would have been a warrior, too. Instead, she was *special*. How could her human mother begin to understand the wildness than ran in her dragon blood? If she had, Grace would never have asked Medellyn to tame her spirit.

Breathing hard, she came to an abrupt halt and screamed into the trees. Her body shook with rage and she tore at the pretty gown she wore. She hated her body, hated being special, hated being expected to act like a lady when she felt like a dragon. Her taloned finger snagged on the crystal around her neck and she cut the leather strap of the necklace. The crystal flew several feet away.

"I am not some man's chattel," she yelled, knowing she'd run far enough away that her mother could not hear her retorts. Since she was shifted her voice was hoarse and powerful, and she reveled in the fierceness of it. "I am not some breeding ceffyl to have children. It is not my place to give you fifty grandkids. I can't help you only had one child. If you would have made me a boy, I wouldn't be a disappointment to you!"

Tears stung her eyes as Medellyn walked aimlessly, searching the forest floor for the fallen necklace. Finding it, she grabbed the inert crystal into her fist. It was a reminder of all she was expected to be. She took a deep breath, looking at her fist and then to the stones littering the forest floor. A small smile formed on her mouth. Medellyn dropped the crystal on the hard ground and glared at it. Rage boiled inside her, the kind of rage surely only a dragon-shifter could feel.

"This is what I think of your fate," she growled as she fell to her knees.

Medellyn grabbed a heavy rock and smashed it down onto her necklace. The crystal cracked. The noise gave her some satisfaction so she hit it again. Grunting with each strike of the stone, she didn't stop until her future had been ground to dust.

"That is what I think of your destiny."

CHAPTER 2

VAR ROYAL PALACE, Eighteen Years Later…

Prince Attor of the Var smiled at Lord Myrddin from across the inner courtyard of the palace where they had come to dine away from the king's hall. Though they were not related, the man was like an older brother to him and sometimes even like a father. Myrddin was well liked in the Var court—especially by the visiting female dignitaries. Though he was shorter than most cat-shifters, his dark hair and eyes seemed to draw the women in. There was an air of power in him that was well deserved. He came from a long line of nobility, one of the old houses.

Like most of the Var palace, the inner court-yard had intricate symmetrical patterns on the walls made of decorative tiles of red, orange, blue, gold and green, with beautifully arched entryways with no doors. There could be no doubt the palace was lavish, but the maze of halls was purposefully confusing to outsiders. The idea had been to disorientate those who should not be wandering the palace alone. Instead, it made for many nights when servants had to be sent out to find some drunken dignitary who'd stumbled around and had become lost.

Attor had proposed installing a central mainframe computer connected to every room. It would not only help the drunks find their way back to their rooms without assistance, but it would monitor their whereabouts. He'd done his research, found a system that could answer vocal queues, track bio-functions, open doors, deliver food and locate anyone programmed into the system by a simple command. But did his father hear him out? No. The king had laughed and waved him out of the dining hall.

Attor looked at the piece of fruit in his hand. He had been told the courtyard had been one of his mother's favorite places and, as a child, it was one of the only ways he could feel her presence. King Auguste loved his son from a distance, and Attor had never known the love of his mother. She'd died giving birth to him—an only son—and King Auguste had never fully recovered from the loss of his life mate. Over the years, the king took other women to his bed, but nothing came from the empty pairings. And, with each passing affair, his father seemed to lose a bit of himself until he was a drunken, hollow shell of a king. Attor resented the weakness his father allowed to show.

Had he bothered to shift into his mountain lion form, he would have been able to hear Myrddin's words over the rush of the water fountain behind him. The fountain was in the center of the room, surrounded by fruit trees and yellow ferns. It was the fruit he had come to dine on, since he was avoiding his father's inebriated conversation.

Myrddin winked at him and smoothed the front of his long nobleman's jacket. Attor gave a small laugh. He didn't need to hear the conversation to know what the man was doing. Myrddin didn't believe in taking only one woman. He wanted several and had made it his roguish mission to have sex with as many women as he could seduce. And the women did come easily, for who were they to say no to money and power. Though not nearly as jaded as his friend, Attor would not turn a willing woman from his bed.

"I thought you were chasing the visiting Azoomian woman," Attor said as Myrddin approached.

Myrddin grinned, reaching to test the firmness of a fat yellow fruit hanging above him. "Mm, she was not as big of a challenge as she would have me believe." He gave the fruit a notable squeeze. "I squeezed her juices from her last night and had to tell her this morning that I would not be making her my lady."

"Did you promise to marry her?" Attor knew it wouldn't have been the first time his friend had used that line.

"Does it matter?" Myrddin laughed and gave the fruit a hard yank, snapping it forcefully from the limb it clung to. The noble tossed it at Attor, forcing him to drop the piece he held to catch it before it hit his face. "Women are like fruit on a tree, to be tasted, enjoyed, and then discarded for the next piece." Myrddin kicked the half-eaten piece across the floor. "Hold one too long and it will be sure to rot in your hand."

"There are many who find happiness with life mates," Attor argued.

"Like your father joining fully to your mother, bowing to her like a besotted fool? I was young, but I still remember how he doted on her. There is your proof that a man cannot bow to a woman and still call himself a man. Women have the potential to be the ruination of men and kingdoms," Myrddin countered. He sighed sadly and shook his head. "Life mating is for peasants who cannot afford many half wives. But you will be king someday,

Attor. Someday soon, if your father continues to keep company with liquor bottles and too much food." He sat and placed his hand on the younger man's shoulder. "To be ruled by a woman is to be ruled by weakness, and kingdoms are only as strong as their rulers. A king must stand alone, beholden to none. When you are king take half mates—many, beautiful half mates. If one dies, you can have sons with the others."

Attor said nothing. This was not the first time Myrddin had tried to convince him of such things. He looked at the fruit in his hand. It was ripe, but it didn't feel as firm as the piece he'd been enjoying before Myrddin had made him drop it. The kings before him had all had one mate and they'd been happy, or so the stories told.

"The king is drunk again, isn't he?" Myrddin let go of Attor's shoulder and leaned his elbows onto his knees.

Attor nodded. "I left when he started challenging the Azoomian noblemen to duels."

Myrddin thought the king pathetic and had often admitted as much to the prince. Attor however just found his father a sad, broken buffoon.

"Enough depression. Let the king have his games. Your time will come soon enough and you can lead this kingdom to greatness. You can give your people the war your father promised us years ago. I'll be by your side, leading your armies, while we defeat those stinking dragon-shifting Draig and take the northern lands as ours. Yours will be a great kingdom, cat-shifters ruling over our slave dragons. Why should they get the mountains when my castle is stuck in the shadowed marshes?"

Attor didn't really care for politics. In fact, they bored him. Wars were tedious and long. He had a palace. What did he want with more land? Then, again, if he was living in the stinking waters of the marshes near the Var-Draig border he might think differently.

"I know what you need," Myrddin said, dropping his voice to a whisper. He reached into his tunic shirt and pulled out a tiny bottle. "I acquired some nef off a couple of marsh farmers."

"You know they're called that because they make their liquor stock out of marsh water, right?" Attor gave a small shiver of disgust.

"But not the nef," Myrddin said. "And the marsh water is purified during the process. Some of it's not bad if you need a quick drunk. But I didn't bring it up to debate alcohol quality. Did you see that Syog beauty I was talking to? A couple of drops of this in her wine, and she'd be game for meeting us in the forest for a chase later. My universal translator is rough when it comes to Syog, but I'm pretty sure she wants light and dark meat."

Myrddin reached to muss up Attor's short blond hair. His friend's eyes shifted with liquid gold. All Var liked the hunt.

Attor's breathing deepened. Nef was illegal and very hard to get. It tamed the cat within them and created restraint in Var men. However, that wasn't why the drug was forbidden. Restraint was fine. Natural restraint without the aid of drugs was better. But, give nef to a humanoid female and it had the opposite effect, making them wild with uncontrolled, indiscriminate passion. When taken together, it would make men's pleasure last longer and women insatiable.

His nostrils flared as if he could already feel the ground beneath his paws. Syogs were not the brightest species, but they were athletic and strong. Unless they were scarred, which many of them were due to their brawling culture, as a whole they happened to be one of the most symmetrically appealing races in the known universes.

The woman Myrddin indicated was phenomenal to look at. Her hair was knotted to the top of her head, but would look marvelously long if she unbound it. She wore the short coat and pleated skirt of her people, and by the look of her naked legs, would be able to run hard and fast. Her dark eyes boldly met his in challenge and, as was the Syog way, she would not look away until he did first.

"What's her name?" Attor asked.

"Does it matter?" Myrddin countered.

"She agrees to take the nef?" Attor swallowed in excitement. A run would do him good, especially if it ended in a hard coupling on the forest floor. "She wants us both?"

"It's settled," Myrddin said by way of an answer. "I'll set it up. Meet me by the flaccid tree in the forest."

Draig Territory, Var-Draig Borderlands

"Mede, I always wanted to ask you. Can you fly?"

Mede grimaced. Saben was clearly well into his cups even though the Order of the Dead Dragons' celebration had only just started. Members of the order had gathered to witness her initiation. Well, that was only half true. They really came for the revelry that would ensue while she ran her trial.

"Well?" Saben insisted.

"No. That's just an old story," she said.

"But you're female," Saben insisted. "If you are

captured tonight, I might not get the chance to ask you again."

"I'm a woman?" Mede gasped in fake shock. She pretended to look down at her body. "That would explain why you proposed to me when we were children."

"Ah, come on, now." Saben leaned forward to whisper, which wasn't really all that quiet—especially considering they were in an encampment of dragon-shifters with incredibly sensitive hearing. "You can tell me the truth. You shift into the dragon of legend, don't you? You can fly." He leaned back, pointing a finger from his goblet-laden hand. "I see it on your face. You can fly."

Mede had been asked this question almost as much as she'd been claimed as a future bride. So, yes, she'd had the dreams. She'd felt her body soaring over strange landscapes. She'd felt her arms as wide as wings. She'd felt the fire of her breath and the lava of her blood. Her body had burned so hot she could barely contain it and knew a human body would never survive with pure dragon blood in it. As far as she could tell, men never had such dreams. Her father seemed to think it was a residual memory from the days long past. Though she'd often caught him watching her when she shifted as a child, as if he'd expected her to take flight.

The dragon legend was from before her people came to Qurilixen, when female dragons were large and fierce and could not take human shape like the men. Their people had no remaining proof of such things, only the stories passed down from each generation, and the fierce creatures depicted boldly in all their artwork and pottery.

"Can you keep a secret?" Mede leaned in to him. Saben nodded. "I can't fly, but you can."

Saben's brow furrowed in confusion. Mede shifted into dragon, slipped her hands beneath the pits of his arms and lifted him upward. In his drunken state and human form he didn't catch what she was doing in time to stop his ascent several feet into the air. He stumbled as he landed on his feet. Then, grinning, he righted himself and held up his goblet. "Not a drop spilled!"

Those who had seen it cheered. Saben went to drink and tipped his head back. He frowned and turned the cup over. It had been empty the whole time. Cheering turned to laughter. Mede couldn't help but chuckle as she went to wash her hands. She loved Saben like a brother, but he sweated like he'd been running around the forest.

"If you want to be one of us, Lady Medellyn, you know what you have to do." Rolant approached and gave her an arrogant half-grin as his eyes lit with challenge.

Mede flung the moisture from her hands and turned to him. She'd known the man for years. They'd trained together as children, and he was to inherit control of the ore mines from his childless uncle. He'd even once claimed he was going to marry her—though that had been years ago. So far, his crystal had never glowed around her, so their relationship was pretty much cemented in friendship.

"The name is Mede," Mede answered. "I don't care if you are a prince, get it right or I'll make you bow to me when I return with my prize."

"You know the initiation rules," Rolant warned, not for the first time. He lowered his voice so the handful of Draig warriors with them couldn't hear. His green eyes shone with concern. "Seriously, Mede, once you cross the borders, we can't come after you. If you get caught you're on your own until your father comes to fetch you."

She said nothing. Having her great warrior father come and rescue her from Var imprisonment would be beyond humiliating, almost as much as getting caught in the first place.

Cynan came close and leaned in. He was a beefy warrior with a fierce demeanor and the playfulness of a naughty child. "What are we whispering about?"

"My brother still wants to meet Mede but she

refuses," Rolant said, before turning his grin to Mede. "He'll be king someday. You can't avoid him forever. I think you two would—"

"Don't make me rip your throat out of your neck," Mede warned.

Cynan laughed. He, too, had tried to claim Mede as a child bride. In fact, she was pretty sure all the Dead Dragons had. To the others, he stated, "I don't envy any man who's unlucky enough to have to claim this dragon."

The men laughed harder and began their good-natured taunting. Since they teased her about her warrior's fierceness, Mede didn't mind it so much.

"He's a good man," Rolant said when Cynan wandered off and could no longer eavesdrop—unless he really wanted to. Shifters had excellent hearing, so it was hard to keep secrets in a small encampment. However, they were honorable dragons and they would respect each other's privacy with little effort. "You can't keep ignoring invitations to the palace forever. You're the only female, Mede. That's—"

"I've never laid eyes on our future king and I don't want to. I have a hard enough time when people with power over me are trying to control me. I don't want to have to defy the orders of your parents, but I am not a pet to be put on display. I respect King Tared and Queen Lorna greatly, from a commoner's distance, but I have no interest in life at court. As for meeting new men, you sound like my mother. She constantly tries to trick me into the presence of new males in hopes their crystals will twitch in my direction, so I'll know before the ceremony who my future is. The men all take alien brides. Why would my fate be different? It's possible that my crystal would have glowed for an offworlder, but I broke it and do not regret doing so. I still have no interest in knowing a husband. Give me a weapon, a good bottle of Qurilixian rum and—"

"Gods' bones, woman," he swore in aggravation. Mede knew he was struggling with the Draig need to protect their females. However, most of the females needed a man's protection because they were humancid. She was a shifter, and this was her chance to prove it once and for all. At least Rolant, and the others in the ancient Dead Dragons order, treated her more equally than most. "Are you sure you want to do this? No one expects you to prove yourself."

"Why?" She stiffened. "Because I'm a woman?"

Rolant turned his eyes away. That was answer enough.

"I'm doing it. I have completed every grueling task demanded of me by the order. And when I get back, you will make me a full member of the Dead Dragons." Mede reached to pull a lock of his light brown hair, forcing him to look at her. At her hard expression, he nodded. Mede let him go. "Good."

Due to the three suns and a single moon revolving around the small planet at different angles, the land was always cast in light, except for once a year, when all suns set at the same time. The light had a green tint that would dim into a bluer hue, in what they considered the evening hours. However, near the border marshes, the trees were much thicker than they were by her mountain home and the green leaves soaked in the many suns' rays becoming wide enough to wear as a hat. This created a false darkness in the shadowed marshes and nearby forest. Her eyes shifted as she looked into the trees, cutting through the shadows as if her gaze was made of light.

"Stay to the east, away from the shadowed marshes and black castle. Givre nests are bad this year. Keep moving. Sniff out a marsh farmer. One should be easy enough to detect. Most of them will be in a dead sleep by now. Stay quiet," Rolant instructed.

Mede nodded.

"I vouched for you. Don't disappoint me." He handed her a knife. Loudly, he proclaimed, "You know what you have to do. Back here by dawn."

The group of Draig all shifted fully and began growling in excitement, cheering her on. They would continue to celebrate as she went off alone.

Mede felt the anticipation of her task pumping in her veins, the danger of it, the thrill, the rush. Her shift came over her like a shiver. Dark brown flesh replaced her tanned skin, growing over her body like a shield beneath her loose pants and tunic shirt. A ridge pushed out from her forehead, shielding her nose and brow, and fangs extended from her mouth.

"Flying would be faster!" Saben yelled.

Lifting the knife in a taloned hand, she grinned. Her words were the gruff sound of the dragon as she declared, "Time to skin a cat!"

Mede darted into the forest, leaving the roars of the men behind her. She couldn't fail. This was her one chance to prove she was worthy of being a dragon. No one would treat her like a mere woman again. And with luck, they'd let her out of the upcoming marriage ceremony.

CHAPTER 3

MEDE SPRINTED through the unfamiliar forest. The danger of being on Var land thrilled her. The marsh air filled her lungs, as it tinged the forest with its nearby decay of plants and animals. If she was to cut to the west, she'd find herself in stagnant water. Her shifter hearing focused on her surroundings, sharply tuned to the environment. An animal slithered in the muddy soil before gliding on the water. Insects buzzed and hummed.

Dead leaves crunched beneath her feet. The noise drew her attention back to her course. The sound created a steady beat, punctuated by her even breath. Mede raced through shadows, leaping over logs, ducking under branches, dodging past hanging moss that clung to the overlarge leaves.

Threads of light shone through the thick tree limbs to create tiny dancing spots.

The stretch of her muscles felt so good that she wanted to run forever. But tonight wasn't about a run. It was about freedom—freedom from being special, freedom from the Breeding Festival happening in a couple of months' time, freedom from destiny and fate and marriage. This was her chance to prove herself a peer of some of the most daring of Draig men.

Dead Dragons were an old brotherhood that started as a secret society. Members were protectors of the crown, trusted to perform any task set before them. They were called Dead Dragons because they were as good as dead, dubbed so for the chances they took. Often those chances were risks that, by all rights, should have killed them. Like most secrets, time and rumors spread and soon stories arose of their noble deeds. The secret society wasn't so secret anymore, though admission into the fold was still challenging and rumors still circulated about their ancient rituals. In reality, since they weren't at war, most of those mystical ceremonies boiled down to drinking and stupid dares.

Running alone through Var territory, the unfamiliar terrain, an unauthorized border crossing, all to take a trophy from an unknown cat-shifter?

Yeah, she was pretty sure that counted as insanely dangerous.

Her mind echoed with the resounding beat of a primal rhythm, an old song played in campsites to while away the hours. It urged her on. Only when she'd run miles inland did she finally stop, leaping up in the air to land in a crouched position hidden by a shrub. She tilted her head, listening for a hint of prey. When she heard nothing, she ran another mile and stopped again. Mede repeated the process until finally she heard the soft, deep snore of a man.

She still clutched the curved knife in her hand. Tracking her prey to where he slept was easy. First, she caught the scent of strong liquor. Next, all she had to do was follow the glow of firelight coming through the forest. The encampment was small. The fire shone from beneath a large metal alcohol still that reeked of poor quality liquor. That's where the smell came from. She covered her mouth. It was overwhelmingly pungent to her shifter senses.

Mede let her human form take over her body. The smell remained strong, but at least now she could breathe without her nose and throat burning quite so badly. Near the fire a Var man slept. It would have been easy to tell what kind of shifter he was, even without knowing she was in Var territory. He stunk of cat and old liquor sweat. It was almost with a sense of disappointment that she crept forward to claim her prize. This beast wasn't a challenge. He was a drunkard passed out in the forest.

Mede stood over him, knife in hand, while glancing over her surroundings. This would never do. She needed him shifted.

Nudging him with the tip of her boot, she tried to wake him up. The Var man grumbled and slapped at her foot. She sighed. Why couldn't she have found a warrior, someone worthy of a fight? With this sad piece of givre dung she wouldn't even get a good scar to show off.

She nudged him again, much harder. "Come on, wake up."

Nothing.

There was no guarantee she'd find another cat-shifter before dawn. She had to take what she could get. She walked the campsite looking for tracks in the dirt. She found several by the dented, old still, but they seemed to go in circles. Frowning, she took the tip of her knife and lightly tapped the metal side. It made a light tink-tink noise.

"Gar-umph-arr!"

Mede jumped in surprise as the Var flailed up from the ground like a wild man. His body shifted into a mangy dark brown cat, then back to dirty man, then to cat once more as if his body couldn't decide which it wanted to be. He breathed heavily, intimidatingly lifting his arms out to the side.

"Not again, dragons. You'll not take a piece of Owain!" Deciding to remain a shifted cat, the drunkard swung his arms violently, claws wielded. He turned in circles, as if a group of Draig surrounded him. Mede noticed the cat had several tufts of fur missing from various parts of his body. Apparently, she was not the first Dead Dragon nominee to find him in the forest. No wonder Rolant pointed her in this direction.

"I just need the fur, Owain," Mede said.

"Get your own, dragon," he slurred. "I know you're after my gold."

Mede looked at the still and then back at the cat-shifter in disbelief. She wasn't sure what the gold was—the liquor or his matted coat.

"Try to knock it over again," he challenged, the gruff words slurred.

Before she could answer, a female scream sounded through the trees. Mede stiffened, instantly shifting to sniff at the air. The liquor once again assaulted her. That's when she realized it was also radiating from the ground. Apparently, the other dragons had knocked his still over on their visits. Okay, that was just mean. The still was probably all this pathetically drunk man had in the world.

"I knew it!" the cat-shifter screeched. He turned his claws toward her as if to point with all fingers.

The female screamed again, sounding terrified. Like the Draig, the Var's genetics were affected by the blue sun's radiation and they normally only had male children. As far as she knew, she was the only female shifter currently on planet. That meant the woman was most likely an alien. Mede thought of her human mother. There was no way she could defend herself from a shifter attack.

The decision instantly made, Mede ran from the campsite to help. The mangy cat yelled taunts at her back, celebrating his fierceness and bravery in scaring her away. "That's right. Tell your dragons not to tussle with Owain!"

She ignored him, knowing he was too drunk to give chase. A new hunt was afoot. Three people ran in the forest. The sound of stumbling feet came from the same general direction of the screams, with two stronger gaits giving chase.

Mede couldn't disguise her approach, so didn't bother to try. She only hoped the pursuers would be so focused on the hunt that they wouldn't hear her until it was too late. The scent of fear filled her nostrils. She was close.

It was not lost on her that she was alone on foreign soil, deep enough inside that the other dragons wouldn't hear her call for help. No one would even think to look for her until well after dawn. She was on her own.

THE THRILL of the chase hammered in Attor's blood, heightening the effects of the stout liquor he'd consumed before starting their games. The woman made a good show of being scared and he almost believed it real. He smelled her adrenaline pumping, heard her cries as Myrddin toyed with her. Though the Syog female had much physical strength, when it came to running in the darkened forest the cat-shifters could have overtaken her by now.

The smell of her was in his nose, fueling his ardor. He had yet to take the nef, not wanting to dull his senses too soon. All the stress he felt inside the palace, watching his father make a fool of himself, melted away. Myrddin knew him well enough to know Attor needed this release.

Everything was heightened. He felt the air moving in his lungs. The earth kissed his feet as he ran over it. Branches poked his hands as he grabbed them to swing over thick fallen logs. This is what a Var lived for. Hunting. Running. Freedom.

A sound caught his attention and he slowed

before changing course. Someone joined their hunt. The fact irritated him and he turned to stop them. What better way to fuel his desires than with a fight?

Whoever it was came toward him at full speed. Within seconds they met as they both leaped through the air into an old campsite clearing. A Draig passed by him and he swung his claws in automatic defense. The move was not well aimed and it glanced off the dragon's arm. The contact would do little damage against the armor of dragon skin.

He landed on the ground and spun to face his opponent. What was a Draig doing in his forest? The dragon mimicked his stance, facing him. Attor breathed deeply, anticipating the fight. No one would fault him for killing a Draig in the Var forest —that was if anyone discovered what he was about to do.

Something stopped Attor from attacking. The dragon smelled of liquor, but beneath that was sweetness.

Attor felt a shiver work over his body. "What are you? You do not stink like the Draig warriors. What was your mother? Are you a hybrid? What are you doing on my land?"

The Draig didn't answer. A stream of light shone from above, revealing long hair. Attor sniffed again. Something about that smell caused his desires to stir, like when a woman was in heat.

A woman?

"You're the dragon girl," he exclaimed, lessening his challenging stance.

The Syog screamed, the sound coming fainter than before.

The dragon woman stiffened. "Release the female."

"The female?" Attor laughed. Now that he knew he didn't face a real threat, he relaxed. He let the shift fade from his features and he stood before her as a man, hoping she would do the same. He wanted to see the rare creature for himself. "Take off the dragon. Then we can have a civilized conversation."

News of the female dragon's birth had filtered its way to the palace when he was a child. He'd always been curious to meet her, but never thought the opportunity would arise. Attor liked rare things, liked collecting them. He thought of the black castle's dungeons. Myrddin would let him keep the dragon woman there like a pet.

"Where are your wings? I thought female dragons could fly." He looked her over. Yes, a fine pet.

She merely stared at him.

"Do you seek asylum here?" he asked. Her

capture might be easy indeed. She'd walk right into her cage.

The Draig woman relaxed. The dark armor of her body rippled, turning from hard shell to supple flesh. The liquid gold in her eyes lessened to reveal gray beneath. Once the ridge pulled back into her face, her brow smoothed. Attor's breath caught. He had not been expecting beauty, yet she was one of the most beautiful creatures he'd ever seen. That surprised him. The Draig were strong, but he didn't expect he'd ever be attracted to one.

"Asylum?" She laughed at him. Her human voice was pretty, but tinged with a hint of mocking sarcasm.

Attor frowned, not liking the reaction. People laughed at his father, not him. "Then why are you here?"

She lifted her knife and touched a long, tapered finger to the tip of the curved blade. "Maybe I've come to skin a cat." She pointed the blade at him. "And maybe you're that cat."

No woman had ever dared speak to him like that. He was a prince after all.

Even so, her boldness excited him. He would never be frightened of a female. Then, glancing around the forest, he realized she might not know who he was. "All these years no Var has claimed to see you. It's speculated they keep you locked away performing strange Draig rituals. Is it true you lay eggs filled with power?"

The woman gave him an unpleasant look. "Is it true Var eat their young?"

It was his turn to express distaste. He grimaced. "Then you need help. That is why you are here."

"Do I look like some damsel locked in a castle?" She stared at him, her gray eyes glinting with gold only to fade again.

"You have a toughness to you." He lifted his hands as if taming a wild animal. "I'm not judging. I just wonder if there is also softness in you."

"You have a softness to you, cat. How about we stop talking and you shift?" She wiggled the blade meaningfully.

He frowned, not liking that she called him soft. "It couldn't have been easy being raised around men with no women like you to teach you gentler ways. A woman who looks like you can't possibly be all hard. Put down the blade and stop trying to threaten me."

She held her arms out to her sides, not dropping the knife but no longer pointing it at him. "Fine. Speak."

The Syog made a strange noise. The woman instantly turned her blade back toward him.

"It is a game," he said. "One she plays willingly."

The dragon didn't look as if she believed him.

"If no Var has knowingly laid eyes on you, I can assume you do not know the Var. We are not what your people make us out to be. I know there are centuries of discord, but we are not at war right now. You have no reason not to trust me. We have no reason to harm women." He tilted his head, trying to listen to what was happening with the Syog. "Use your ears. Do you hear them?"

Slowly the woman nodded. "What are they doing?"

Attor grinned. It was clear to him the Syog had just been caught and Myrddin was in the throes of wild sex. Ah, so the dragon was kept innocent. This pleased him. Perhaps he would not lock her in a cage as a pet.

Attor was glad he hadn't drunk the nef. The pleasure that welled inside him was fierce and strong. Already heightened by a chase, his cat begged him to play. His eyes roamed her human form with renewed interest as she concentrated on the noise. Hearing Myrddin and the alien woman only aroused his ardor more.

"They're..." Attor let a smile curl his lips. A low, seductive laugh escaped him. "They are coupling."

"Oh," she answered, followed by a more surprised, "Oh! So they are married."

Yes, innocent. It was so clear now.

"No. She's visiting the palace," he said.

"From space?" The woman frowned. "I heard your people like to invite aliens to the planet. Don't you think it would be better if they just left us alone? Why make them so welcome as to run freely about the land?"

"They do leave you alone. They stay in Var territory. Besides, your people meet with aliens."

"Only the Mining Ambassador for trade."

"Your marriage ships," he pointed out.

"Yeah, those, too." She didn't seem too enthused by the idea. "That part can't be helped, but at least it's only once a year. Though, I suppose you don't have anything to do with the decision to allow aliens to land on Var territory. Everyone knows the king likes the company since his wife passed."

"Explain yourself," Attor said, stiffening at the mention of his father.

"Losing a mate can't be easy. I've seen what happened to the elders who lost their wives. It's sad."

Attor relaxed by small degrees. She clearly didn't know who he was.

When she wasn't threatening his hide, the woman had a regal beauty worthy of royalty. She possessed those things that could not be taught—

attitude, confidence, a noble bearing—all of which were evidence of a superior class. The fact that she was a shifter made her powerful. Her Draig heritage made her rare. No one on his planet, or in any of the known universes, possessed a dragon-shifter wife. She was the only one of her kind alive. And, her innocence had yet to be claimed.

Why had he not considered her before? He'd just assumed her dragon blood would have made her mannish and permanently covered in scales. Such was not the case.

"And to only have one son?" she continued. "I am an only child because my mother is a descendent of a delicate people. I know how my parents wish it was different. They try to hide it, but I know. I imagine the Var prince must feel much the same. I am just glad I am not in line to rule a kingdom."

Women didn't need to rule kingdoms. That was not their role.

"The forest is no place for a maiden," Attor said, feeling very protective of her. But it was more than that. He wanted her. And why should he not have her? He was heir to the Var throne. Someday he would rule half the planet—*all* of the planet if Myrddin had his way. He would need a queen worthy of being on his arm.

"I can take care of myself," she answered.

Fierce and innocent and compassionate. It all

made perfect sense. Fate surely had a hand in this night's adventure. Their meeting was a sign of things to come. He would possess her. This woman would be his bride.

"Why are you looking at me like that?" Mede asked the cat-shifter. It's not like she'd revealed any great secrets. Everything she'd said about her family was common knowledge amongst her own people.

Curiosity got the better of her. She'd never spoken to a Var before, and this one seemed civilized in manners. The man was handsome, but so were most of the shifters she'd been around. His short blond hair had been recently trimmed, and he clearly had immaculate grooming habits. The stories she'd heard of the cats were of uneducated, dirty beasts with forked tongues and dark hearts roaming like feral beasts. There was a reason the Draig avoided coming into the southern marshlands that edged the borders. Geography lessons had taught her that not all Var territory was marsh, but she'd always had the impression that the good land belonged to the Draig.

"You're staring at me," she said when he didn't answer. The man's pants were tight and his shirt fitted against the muscles in his chest. She'd noticed cross-lacing up the back of his spine. The strings held the material together, while still allowing a peek of flesh along the man's back. The Draig tended to wear looser pants and pullover tunic shirts that better accommodated the dragon-shift.

"You are exquisite," he answered simply. His eyes glowed. She recognized the fierceness in him. She carried it, too. "What is your name?"

That surprised her. "You don't already know?"

Whoever this man was, he didn't look at her like other men did. The Var didn't have crystals, but relied on more primitive methods for finding a mate. It was a relief to meet a man who was not obsessed with her marriage. Normally, within two seconds they were checking their necklaces to see if they were the one, trying to not-so-sneakily get closer to her, as if that would help. A few had even tried to make her hold their stones as if her touch would activate them.

Several minutes had passed and not once had the cat-shifter mentioned the will of the gods and fated mates. This fact alone made her inclined not to slice off a piece of him for the Dead Dragon challenge just yet. She sighed. The hour crept closer to dawn and she still needed to make the run back.

"You're not going to tell me?" the man laughed. "Fair enough. I won't tell you who I am."

The sounds of the distant love-play lessened. The cat-shifter had been moving forward very slowly as they talked. He probably thought she hadn't noticed when in fact she'd watched his every move without looking directly at him. There was liquid grace in his movements, something the tougher Draig warriors lacked. Every gesture was like an invitation to dance.

"Will you at least tell me what you're doing in our forest?" he inquired.

"I already did. I have to skin a cat." She lifted the knife and swayed it back and forth.

"I am afraid I can't allow that."

"I am afraid I am not asking for your permission." She liked that he challenged her. In many ways his attitude was a relief. "All I need is a tuft of fur and then I can go back. Failing in my task is not an option."

The cat smiled. He lifted up his arm and let a partial shift overcome his flesh. Fur sprouted on skin. The light blond suited his coloring.

Mede didn't need further invitation. She shaved a strip of hair off his arm with the knife, holding her hand beneath his arm to catch the short fur. As she balled it into a fist she was about to thank him when the man surprised her by leaning forward to press his mouth to hers. She stiffened in shock at the bold move. He grabbed her head with one hand and pulled her tightly to his lips. She felt her knife meet flesh, though she hadn't tried to cut him.

Men often bragged they would be her chosen mate, but never had they been so bold as to kiss her. He parted his warm lips, but she didn't move to return the gesture. The feel of him was more shocking than unpleasant, though there was no mad rush inside her to return the kiss. When finally he released her, he whispered, "You have your token and I have mine."

Mede swallowed nervously. The cat looked at his cut arm unconcerned. A thin trail of blood trickled over his forearm to his fingers. It might leave a scar, but it was not a serious injury.

"I will be seeing you very soon, little dragon." His eyes lit as he backed away from her. "But for now you had better hurry home."

Mede stumbled away from him as if he'd kicked her. The sensation of the kiss warmed her mouth, but she'd been too shocked by the suddenness of it to react. By all rights she should have done more than cut him. To her shame, even the small wound had been by accident. Instead, she'd frozen. A handsome man had kissed her and she'd frozen.

A small price to pay for getting what I came for.

The cat-shifter was right. It was late and she needed to run for the borders.

"That way." He pointed toward Draig territory. "Keep straight. Avoid the still farmers. They soak in so many fumes they're always drunk and erratic."

Mede wiped her mouth with the back of her hand.

"Who are you?" she wondered aloud, wanting to at least know the name of the man who'd first dared to kiss her.

"I'm the man you'll be thinking about until we meet again," he said confidently.

Mede opened her mouth to retort but the man leaped into the air, shifting before his hands found the aid of a branch to swing out of the tiny clearing. She heard his steps taking him away from her. Closing her lips, she looked down at her fur-filled hand. It was a good thing he'd left. She wasn't sure what her retort would have actually been.

"WHERE'S THE SYOG?" Attor asked, glancing around the forest. He caught up to Myrddin next to the flaccid tree. Age and moss had taken its toll on the large limbs, pulling them down so they arced toward the ground rather than up to the heavens.

"She had to catch a flight." Myrddin stretched his arms over his head. Dirt marred his clothes and he had a satisfied look on his face.

"I didn't think the Syog were leaving so soon." Attor frowned. He'd been looking forward to releasing the tension in his loins. By the patterns on Myrddin's knees the man had taken the Syog from behind like an animal. A shiver worked over Attor at the thought. He would have enjoyed seeing the rough ride.

Meeting the dragon woman had surged his already heated ardor and he wanted to sink himself into something soft and warm. As badly as he wanted to fuck his future queen, he saw the wider scope. If she was worthy of marrying him, she was worthy of seduction. The kiss had been merely a way to mark her as his. The gesture had worked, for she'd been weak-kneed afterwards.

Myrddin scratched his waist. "What happened to you? Please tell me you didn't lose the trail."

"Another matter came up," he said, not really wanting to share about his future queen just yet. Myrddin might not approve of his plan.

"More important than a hunt?" His friend shook his head in disbelief. "If you wanted to find a still farmer we could have taken a drink together afterwards." Myrddin lowered his gaze to look at

Attor's tunic and sniffed at him. "If you couldn't wait for a drink…"

Attor knew there was a faint trace of liquor on his body from the woman who'd clearly been next to a still. The smell had permeated her clothing.

Myrddin lifted his fist in warning. "I will beat you before I let you become weak like your father."

Attor slapped the hand away. "I'm not my father. If you must know I was setting events into place that will help when I take over the throne."

"Oh?" Myrddin arched a brow. At least he was no longer looking at him in disappointment.

Against his better judgment, he explained, "I've decided to take the Draig female as my queen."

Myrddin physically recoiled at the idea.

"I just met her. She's beautiful, and—"

"You let a Draig escape?" Myrddin demanded. His eyes shifted and he tilted his head. "Where is she? Which way did she run?"

"No. Let her go." Attor didn't want Myrddin near the woman. "I have plans for her."

"What plans could you possibly have for Lady Medellyn?" Myrddin demanded. "Unless it's to torture her to start a war?" Suddenly, the man nodded. "We could kidnap her and make a very public show of her suffering. That will be an act the Draig cannot ignore."

Medellyn. That was her name? He hid his smile.

"No." Attor tried to turn his friend's bloodlust against him. "Think of how much easier it will be for me to take the northern territories if I'm married to their only female. If she chooses me over any of them. If she bows to me, her husband and king, before all others." The idea excited him. He would be the sole possessor of the rarest of creatures. She would be his. She would love him. She understood his position as an only child, meant to rule. She had compassion for his drunk of a father. Attor clung to those facts. "Together we will rule the entire planet."

Myrddin grinned. "Yes. Together we will rule."

Attor had meant himself and his bride, but didn't correct the man.

"Well done, son, well done," Myrddin slapped him hard on the shoulder. Then, nodding downward to where Attor's body showed the evidence of his unfulfilled night, he added, "Come. Let us find you a servant to suck the poison from you. I promise on the next hunt you can go first."

CHAPTER 4

MEDE'S LUNGS expanded with the effort of a hard run. Morning crept over the horizon, brightening the night. In one hand she gripped Rolant's knife, and in the other, her prize. For a moment, she felt perfection in the burn of her legs, the pant of her breath, the rhythm of her feet. When she jumped over forest debris, she flew.

The exercise felt wonderful, but not nearly as wonderful as the sounds of cheers coming from the border. They had lit a fire to guide her back and she ran toward it. As she neared the group of dragons she leapt over the border. Lifting her hand, she yelled, "Dragons!"

"Dragons!" the men returned loudly, celebrating her victorious run.

Mede turned the hilt of the knife toward

Rolant to return the blade. He took it. Instantly, his smile faded as he saw the blood. His eyes roamed her as she let the dragon-shift fade from her body. Before he could ask her about it, she proudly lifted her fist balled around the fur. "Victory!"

"Victory!" The men cheered, clearly well into their cups. While she'd had her adventure, they'd partied.

"Our lady found the still," Arthur said with a laugh, as he sniffed the liquor fumes on her. The man had a crook to his nose from having been punched a few too many times. When he drank, he liked to brawl.

"How is the mangy cat?" Cynan asked.

"Owain remembers you fondly," Mede answered, grinning. A round of shouts and laughter cut off the conversation. After it finally died down, she held out her hand. "My prize."

A few of the men looked down at her outstretched hand, then a couple more. Their laughter died as they took in her achievement.

"That doesn't look like..." Saben gave her a questioning look.

Dylan reached to pinch a bit of the fur. "It's blond."

"Mede?" Rolant inquired, clearly wishing she'd explain. "Didn't you find the still?"

"Yes, but I wanted a harder target," she said.

"Besides, the still farmer was already missing a lot of tufts. I felt sorry for him."

Rolant lifted the blade, showing the blood to the others. "Who did you fight?"

Mede thought of the stranger. There was no reason to tell them what had happened. They didn't need to know the cat-shifter had kissed her. That would be her secret.

"We didn't exchange names." She gave a little shrug of dismissal.

"Test it, so none may challenge her claim," Rolant said. There was a lot of fumbling as they searched for a particular satchel that held the genetic testing fluid. As the others were distracted, Rolant pulled her aside. "I sent you to the still farmer. What were you thinking? The only blond Var I have seen belong to the elite palace guards. Or to the prince. How did you get it? Why is there blood on—?"

"It's good!" Dylan yelled, lifting a small vial to pour testing liquid onto the ground. When the cat-shifter fur combined with the chemicals it turned the test liquid a pale blue. "It's Var."

"Not now, Rolant," Mede said. "I need a drink."

A bottle was instantly shoved in her direction. She drank deeply of the liquor. It stung her throat and warmed her belly.

"Tell us of the run," Cynan said.

"What's this?" a male voice boomed over the encampment.

Mede was relieved, for it saved her from having to tell that particular fireside story.

"Do you have permission to be on my land?" the stranger continued.

Mede lowered the bottle and wiped her mouth on her sleeve. She didn't recognize the voice. Several of the men blocked her view. Since they were camped on palace land with Prince Rolant she wasn't too concerned by the claim.

"Brother," Rolant acknowledged. "You've returned. I thought you were hunting yorkins."

"Gildas was injured. Nothing serious, but we decided to bring him home so he could have the proper medical attention," Prince Llyr answered.

Mede changed her mind. She didn't like the interruption. This was her victory morning. She didn't want to meet a new male Draig, and certainly not the prince who was heir to the throne. The prince was not married and had already told Rolant he wanted to meet her.

"Hand me a drink," Llyr said. "Whose victory are we celebrating?"

Like grass being blown aside by a stout wind, the men parted to let Llyr see her. She stiffened and automatically lifted her jaw. "Mine."

"You?" Llyr repeated in disbelief. He looked at Rolant for confirmation. "And she passed?"

"And we saw her fly," Saben inserted.

"That was you who flew," Arthur said.

"Oh, right." Saben nodded. He lifted his cup and announced. "And *I* flew!"

"How is Owain?" Llyr asked.

"In need of a bath," Mede said.

"She brought back blond fur," Rolant stated.

"Blond…?" Llyr handed the bottle he held to his brother and stepped forward to look at her.

Mede was glad she smelled like a liquor still and sweat. And she probably looked like a wild beast after her run. She forced herself not to glance at his chest to see his crystal. Looking at his face was worse.

In many ways he reminded her of Rolant, only his eyes were a brighter green—so bright they penetrated her, taking her in as if he could see all her secrets. Mede didn't like to feel exposed. His light brown hair hung to his chin whereas Rolant's was much longer. She thought of the kiss the Var had stolen from her. She had not been expecting it and really had felt nothing but surprise when it happened, but the memory caused her eyes to dart down to Llyr's mouth.

"Finally we meet, Lady Medellyn," he said.

Mede forced her eyes away from his firm lips.

She swallowed nervously. "I am called Mede. And I am not a lady. Today I am a Dead Dragon."

At the words the inebriated men cheered. "Dead Dragons!"

Llyr chuckled. More to himself than to her, he said, "I can see the liquor has not gone to waste here."

"If you'll excuse me, prince, I earned the Dead Dragons' mark and I want my scar." She made a move to leave his presence, still refusing to look down. The idea that a prince would be her mate terrified her. She'd never wanted this meeting.

"Wait," Llyr said, being so bold as to grab her arm. "I should like to congratulate you on a good run."

Mede arched a brow. The more she found herself mesmerized by his eyes, the more stubborn her demeanor became. When he didn't speak, she said, "Well?"

"Congratulations on a good run," he said softly.

"Thank you, prince," she answered dutifully before moving to skirt past him. The men had started to sing a bawdy song as they linked arms and began a noisy, drunken chain through the campsite. The prancing took them away from where she stood. She wished they'd circle back.

Llyr grabbed her arm again. "Did you really take the fur from a member of the royal court?"

At the time she hadn't been nervous, but now, the way both Llyr and Rolant mentioned the fur's color, made her suddenly a little sick to her stomach. Nerves bunched in her chest and she nodded once. "I suppose I did, though at the time I didn't ask for his name."

"What did he look like?"

"A cat," she answered, being difficult on purpose. His fingers lingered on her arm, the touch somehow intimate. Finally she got the nerve to look down. At first, she thought she might have seen a soft glow in the stone. She stiffened, until she realized that it must have been firelight reflection. He was not her mate. A sigh of relief whispered past her lips...followed by a sense of disappointment. The disappointment confused her and made her want to run away like a coward.

"Have you mated?" Llyr asked, eyeing the lack of crystal around her neck.

Always to that.

She lowered her eyes over her lashes. "I have no interest in marriage. I would like my scar though.' She tried to pull her arm.

He tightened his grip. "So it is true. You broke your own crystal. Why?"

Mede grimaced, remembering that day long ago. Her mother had wept openly for months over it. "So did you." She reached for his chest, pinching the crystal from where it laid against him and gave it a little toss. It bounced against him. An almost microscopic thin crack marred the inside of the stone.

"An accident when I was a boy trick-riding ceffyls," Llyr said.

"My father is a ceffyl breeder. You should not be trick-riding them," she lectured. "They are in delicate supply and not for games."

"I was a boy," he stated, enunciating the words. His attitude infuriated her.

"No excuse," she answered just as arrogantly.

"I broke my arm, if that helps."

"It's a start." She again tried to pull her arm free from his grasp. Tiny shivers worked along her skin where he touched her, a strange vibration that compelled her to focus on the contact.

The singing had reached the forest and the men disappeared behind a colossal tree. Somehow being alone with him made her nervous.

"Unhand me, prince," she said at last. "I earned my place here."

Llyr looked at her arm in surprise, as if he didn't know he held her. Instantly his fingers released her. "Tell me first, why did you crush your crystal?"

"What? I love me. I married myself." She wasn't sure why she was being obstinate or sarcastic. All she knew was that her arm tingled where he'd touched her. She glanced at his stone. It didn't glow. Still, the urge to run from him was great. Her muscles felt weak. Surely her body shook from the long night of exercise, nothing else. Her mind felt fuzzy because she was tired. It had nothing to do with his smell or those eyes. Those damned green eyes.

"Somehow I don't think you're truly that narcissistic, my lady."

"Very well. If you must know, it is because I make my own fate." Mede gave a little hop past him and went to join the dancing men. Saber and Cynan broke the chain to let her in. As they pulled her away from the prince, she was glad for the escape. Something about the man drew her in and frustrated the netherworld out of her. She was pretty sure it was his eyes. No man should ever possess eyes like that.

LLYR COULDN'T BREATHE AS he watched the woman dance away from him. Mede smelled horrible with sweat plastering her hair and dirt marring her check. But there was a sparkle in her eyes that made all the other imperfections fade into nothing.

She was exactly as fierce as he'd remembered

her being from that day, long ago, when he'd seen her in the forest. He'd always wanted to officially meet her, but something inside him had told him to wait. And he had waited, for nearly twenty years he'd waited.

No one would believe his limited childhood powers of divination, but Llyr had been born with the innate knowledge that he would marry a woman like her. Ever since he was a small boy he'd dreamed of finding his mate in another shifter. When he was older, one glimpse of Mede had confirmed it. He'd been too young at the time to actually receive the will of the gods and his crystal had not glowed. But he had known. Deep inside, he had known. He didn't need a crystal to tell him as much. For many years he'd clung to a fleeting moment. Even now the smell of the mountain forest stirred that memory.

Llyr never imagined seeing her again would make those feelings he carried inside him grow, and that he could feel as strongly toward her as he did this night. Yes, he'd had his moments of doubt. Twenty years was a long time to carry a torch for a woman he'd only seen once. But it had been worth it. Everything he needed to know was confirmed when he looked at her.

"So what did you think of our female dragon?" Rolant asked. "Didn't I tell you she was beautiful?

Ah, but that beauty comes with a set of sharp teeth. She can take a bite out of any man and hold her own against any warrior. I don't envy the man who is fated by the gods to be her mate."

Instead of answering, Llyr reached into his pocket and took out his crystal. He lifted it for Rolant to see without needing to verify things for himself. Rolant gave a small gasp and turned to look at where Mede danced around the bonfire with the others.

"But…?" Rolant looked at Llyr's chest to the dormant crystal he wore.

"I have been sending her invitations to the palace under our mother's name for months now, but she always finds an excuse, or simply hides so the runners can't find her. You have told me how she feels about marriage," Llyr said. "I took your warnings to heart. This stone belongs to Gildas." The palace servant had been only too happy to lend his necklace to a prince, thinking it would add to his luck. Honor dictated that the sacred object would be returned undamaged. Well, as undamaged as it had been when Llyr had received it. "He's injured and has no present use for it. Since he doesn't believe in medical units, he'll be mending for some time."

"Why wouldn't you let her know who you are to her?" Rolant frowned. "Hand me Gildas' stone and put yours on. Let her see it. You can stop her from getting the brand of the Dead Dragon."

"I will not change her path until the gods officially bless us." Llyr tucked his own stone back into his pocket. "Who am I to interfere with the future queen's fate?"

"Uh, you are the future king?" Rolant stated the obvious.

Llyr gave a small laugh. "You saw that fur. She earned her scar. If I take that away from her now she'll never have me." He smiled and it was hard to hide his excitement. "You do not dictate orders and expect to win a woman like that. If I get possessive, if she knows who I am to her, she'll never make it to the next Breeding Festival. I need her at the festival. The gods will take care of the rest."

Rolant frowned. "How would you know how to win a woman like that? There are no other women like that."

"Because I know dragons and I know the warrior spirit. Those who join the Order of the Dead Dragons are of a special breed. No one in this encampment could be won or persuaded by force." Llyr watched Mede dance by. Her eyes met his and he slowly nodded to acknowledge her. It was all he could do not to dance after her.

She was a truth that had filled his every moment. He'd waited his entire lifetime for her. But that knowledge had not prepared him for the gut-slamming, heart-squeezing, loin-filling reality that was Lady Mede. Even now he could feel her against his fingers. The nerves in his hand tingled, sending tiny shockwaves of awareness through his body. By some unknown willpower he held himself back and watched the sway of her hips and the blowing of her hair. Llyr knew the gods were always testing them to ensure they were worthy of the blessings bestowed.

"Mark her as she wishes. Let her join the order. These men will become her brothers and will protect her with their lives," Llyr said.

"You will perform the marking?" Rolant asked. "Tradition says the highest rank must cut the flesh."

Llyr could not harm Mede. To do so, even when requested, went against every protective instinct growing inside him. "No. I will leave. You do it." He took a deep breath. "Just make sure she doesn't do any more dangerous missions. Dragon or not, the borderlands are no place for a woman. We may not officially be at war, but the Var king is a puppet and the old house lords do as they please. They will not honor any peace if they get one of ours alone."

"I tried to stop her," Rolant defended. "Of course I tried to stop her. I gave her the most disgustingly hard tasks I could think of leading up to this night. She did them all without complaint. When that didn't work, I directed her to the still where the easy target sleeps off his drunken stupor. Her father is a great warrior and well respected. I couldn't turn down her attempts without reason. I don't know how she found someone from the Var palace tonight. The forest near the marshes should have been empty. They smell of death and tree rot. No one goes there unless forced, or they're farming illegal ale. There are no Var festivals this time of year to drive them to the trees."

Llyr placed his arm on his brother's shoulder. "She is safe. That is what matters. But now that you know she is your future sister and queen, perhaps keep a closer watch on things. The whole of our kingdom's future rests in her."

THE WHOLE of Attor's future happiness rested with the dragon woman, his future queen. Attor closed his eyes to the long stretch of forest, the view visible from his private balcony. It encased a small lake and led toward distant mountains. A soft breeze caressed him, tickling him through the cross laces running up the back of his shirt. Being that the balcony was high off the ground, no one below in the palace yard could see him, though if he leaned over the rail he could hear them walking about below.

Attor gave a low moan and gripped the liquor bottle he held tighter. The sound caused the woman on her knees before him to quicken her mouth's pace and suck harder. His breathing deepened.

Already he could feel Medellyn's love for him, her adoration. How could it be otherwise? He felt his destiny in her.

Attor opened his eyes. Soon all this land would be his. Medellyn would be a fine queen. They would have many strong sons, half-cat, half-dragon, a new fierce breed to take over the planet. The Draig gene would be recessive, of course, as cat-shifter genes were obviously better and stronger.

More than that, Medellyn had the capacity to love him. She *would* love him. And he would love her. Her strength was in her heritage. She was strong. She would not die in childbirth like his mother had. He would never have to be alone.

Attor glared down at the woman on her knees before taking a drink from the stout liquor. The pleasure of her mouth faded when he looked at her face. The eyes staring up at him were blue, not gray. And her hair was red, not black. With his free hand he grabbed the back of her head and held her on his shaft. Regardless of his displeasure in her looks, he found release. The pressure inside his stomach eased and he groaned, closing his eyes tight to imagine his future bride.

"Come, wench," the watching Myrddin said as Attor tied his laces. The man lounged against the stone and iron railings along the balcony's edge. The green-blue sky of morning shone on his excited face. He began unfastening his pants. The woman stood without question and went to the nobleman. As Attor moved to go inside to his palace bedroom, Myrddin turned her toward the railing and continued to free himself.

Attor stumbled through the door. The balcony exit was inside his enormous closet. He paused long enough to pull off his shirt and toss it on the floor for the maid to get when she was done. He glanced out the long, rectangular window on the exterior wall opposite his numerous racks of clothing. Myrddin was lifting the woman's skirts to take her from behind. Attor watched the show for a few moments.

"Tell me it's the best cock you've ever had in you," Myrddin commanded, clearly not realizing Attor listened from just inside the balcony door. "All men pale in comparison to its big, fat size, don't they? Call me your king. Call me your king!"

The woman obeyed, but probably not with the

enthusiasm Myrddin wanted because the man growled and pounded her harder. Attor was too tired and too drunk to care how Myrddin found release.

The prince pushed through the bedroom door and instantly went toward the bed. A fire had been lit in the marble fireplace, the maid's task before she'd been urged to her knees. The decadence of the large room with the smooth stone floor, woven rugs and golden decorations was lost on him. Falling face first toward the mattress, he was met with soft sheets and instantly went to sleep.

MEDE GRITTED her teeth as the dragon symbol was cut into her lower back. She felt the pour of liquor on her exposed shoulder. It trickled down, stinging the wound Rolant made with the special marking knife. The heated blade had been formed to make the Dead Dragon symbol, so that all the deep cuts could be made and cauterized at once to produce a scar. She was not allowed to shift and had to endure the pain as her human self.

"Agh," she screamed as liquor hit the wound a second time. Her tunic shirt was pulled up in the back so Rolant could work, but did not expose her immodestly to the others. The liquor wet her pants.

At that moment she didn't care if her clothes reeked of a brewery and were stained with her dripping blood. This morning marked the beginning of her new life—a life of freedom and respect. She breathed hard, taking the pain she'd fought so arduously for. The men cheered, saying their congratulations in warrior grunts and tired jesting —all but Saben who had fallen asleep face down in the dirt about an hour before.

"It's over," Rolant whispered in her ear as he handed the blade to Arthur for safekeeping. Someone pressed a bandage to her back and pulled her shirt down.

Mede found herself looking for Llyr, but knew if Rolant cut her the man had not stayed to see her ceremony. She felt slighted by his disappearance.

"I've got a medical unit in my tent. I won't heal the wound, but I can take away the pain." Rolant pulled at her elbow to help her stand.

"No special treatment. I am a brother of the order now. I will act accordingly," Mede said.

"I don't think we've ever had a female. I think you're a sister of—"

"I said what I meant. I'm no different than any man here." Mede pulled away from him and slowly walked toward her tent to sleep. The bright light of morning shone around her, like a rebirth, as her new brothers found their ways into intoxicated dreams. She drew back the flap and crawled onto the mound of furs on the floor. A groan left her as she lay on her stomach. Mumbling, she tried to ignore the tingling in her arm where the prince had touched her, as she swore, "I don't care that you didn't stay to witness my honor, Prince Llyr. You weren't invited tonight anyway. Go back to your palace and touch me no more."

CHAPTER 5

Draig Northern Mountains, Medellyn's Family Home

Mede averted her eyes. The sound of her mother's tears was the only thing that could make her feel guilty, no matter how she tried to act like she didn't care what anyone thought of her. Everything her mother did was delicate and sweet. Her voice was low and gentle, as if she always comforted a sick child with it. Small hands never hit with force, not even when kneading dough. When she cried it was soft sobs and little noises of disappointment that tore at her daughter's heart.

Of course Mede knew Lady Grace would not like her new brotherhood. In fact, it had been her intention not to tell her mother, and hope that everyone who knew the woman would think better than to gossip about it. Apparently, not everyone had the common sense to keep the news quiet.

"Mother," Mede said, brushing back a strand of dark hair that matched her own. She touched her mother's shoulder. Though people said that when standing still, Mede physically looked like a younger version of Grace, when the women moved and talked, their demeanors made them very different. Mede was aggressive and stubborn, whereas Grace was gentle and reserved. "I bring honor to the family name. The order is one of the oldest on the planet."

Grace took a deep breath. She picked up a plate of sugared biscuits and fussed with arranging them as she walked from the table toward the kitchen. "If it is so honorable, why are its dealings so secretive? And I heard they cut their members. We had gentlemen clubs on my home world. There is a reason women were not allowed to join."

The cut on Mede's back no longer hurt, but the wound was still scabbed. She refused to confirm that part to her mother. With luck, the woman would never see the scar. For all her years surrounded by dragon-shifters and wild spirits, Grace still maintained an innocent quality bred into her during her youth.

Grace was born on one of the Florencian moons, a living-museum settlement locked in what her mother called the Old Earth Victorian era. The settlement did not use space technology, but Old Earth mechanical tools—what she likened to the great-great-great-grandfather of modern advancement. This simple existence had prepared Grace to be a bride on a planet whose people also chose to live simply. However, what Qurilixen did not offer the gentlewoman was the same impossibly high standard of social customs and rules she'd adhered to in the settlement. From the stories Mede had heard of her mother's past, she highly doubted the gentlemen clubs were quite as fierce as being a Dead Dragon.

"I don't think you can compare your gentlemen sitting around talking politics and drinking pea," Mede said. She instantly wished she could take the words back. They'd just kind of slipped out of her mouth.

"*Tea*," her mother stressed with a weary sigh. "The drink was called tea."

"Are you sure?" Mede furrowed her brow. That's not how she remembered it.

"Yes. I'm sure."

"The princes belong to the order," Mede asserted, hoping to lighten her mother's expression. "You said you liked Rolant."

"The princes? Both princes?" That perked her up a little.

"Yes." Mede nodded. "Prince Llyr as well."

"Then you met the heir prince?" Grace asked, not bothering to hide her hopeful tone.

"Yes." Mede again nodded. She thought of the man who constantly danced through her thoughts. There was no reason he should be there, but he was. The fact annoyed her more than her mother's desire to see her wed and pregnant. "I met Prince Llyr. He was very kind."

"And?" Her mother forgot her tears. "Did you go to the palace? Did you see the king's court? Were the palace guards there?"

"No. I met the heir prince at the campsite." Instantly, Mede knew her mistake.

"Campsite? You slept out of doors?" Her mother gave a delicate shiver. She again took a deep breath. Her hand trembled.

"Nothing improper happened. It was on palace grounds." Mede thought of the cutting, of the drunken dancing weaving through the tents, of Llyr's touch on her arm, of getting the Var fur. The Var fur? How could she have forgotten getting kissed by the cat-shifter? Surly a kiss should have ranked higher in her thoughts than a touch on her arm. Grace watched her carefully. Mede smiled brightly. Gods forgive her for lying to her mother. "I promise. I held myself like a lady."

"What did the prince say to you? Are you invited to the palace?" her mother asked.

Did the woman never give up? Mede suppressed her sigh. "We did not speak long. What does an heir prince have to talk about with me? He congratulated me on my honor."

"There was nothing else?" Grace insisted.

"Nothing of importance." Mede thought of his hand on her arm. Even now she could feel the tingling. Her mind's obsession with that touch was weird considering the evidence of his dormant crystal. Perhaps years of her mother's daydreaming had finally rotted into her brain. She was imagining a connection where there was none because he was a prince.

"And the other men of the order," her mother pried, sniffing lightly.

"All kind men who treat me as they would a sister." Mede hoped that would give her mother some comfort. She always talked about how she wished she could give Mede siblings, and how her inability to have more children was her life's regret.

Grace touched Mede's dark hair, running the backs of her fingers over the length of it. "You are so beautiful, my daughter. On my home world you would have been celebrated with fine society parties and afternoon callings. Men would have asked your father's permission to escort you on carriage rides."

It was a fantasy Mede had heard often. When her mother spoke, her eyes glazed and her mind drifted far away. If not for the settlement disbanding, Grace would never have left her Victorian world. For a moment her mother's serene mask slipped to reveal her loss and an intense sadness washed over Mede.

"Do you wish you could have stayed? You never talk of what happened or why the settlement disbanded." Mede placed her hand on her mother's to stop her from needlessly rearranging the biscuits.

"There is no reason to relive unpleasant memories," Grace said. Mede could see her mother did relive it despite the words. She wanted to ask what had happened, but knew not to pry. This was one story her mother kept to herself. Mede wasn't even sure her father knew the truth of it.

"Do you regret coming here?"

Grace blinked back her private thoughts. She instantly shook her head in denial. "Never. Not for one second have I regretted coming here. I love your father more than my own soul. And you, you are my beautiful daughter. I regret not being able to show you my world, how grand ladies were there, but I never regretted having you. You and your father are my life. Without you I am not whole."

"I'm sorry I can't be the lady you want me to be," Mede said.

"The pull of the dragon is strong." Her mother nodded in understanding. "I wish you could feel the human in you as you do the dragon. You give that side so much attention. I want more..." Grace swayed on her feet.

"Mother?"

"It's nothing. I'm tired." Grace smiled weakly. Her words became a little breathless as she tried to act like nothing had happened. "I want so much for you. I want you to feel your human soul. I want you to feel what it's like to have a woman's heart. You in love and married, would make my life complete and I would have nothing left to do in this universe."

Mede eyed her mother's pale face, worried. "I want you to see a medic."

"No. It's nothing." She shooed her daughter's hand away. "I'm just a little tired."

"Mother, seriously. For me," Mede put forth sternly. "If you don't, I'll tell father."

"Don't bother him with nonsense. He has so much to worry about with the herds." Her mother walked away from her, fidgeting with the array of decorative old weapons her father kept hanging on the wall. They were family heirlooms, the blades dulled from centuries of use. The woman's hand moved slowly, not really doing anything useful. She kept her face from view.

"What can I do to get you to see a medic? Name it." Mede watched her mother's back, imagining that she looked thin, too thin. Knots of worry bunched in her stomach. Grace had always been delicate. With the Draig natural lifespans, death was not something Mede thought a lot about. She never considered her parent's mortality before. What was her mother hiding from her? Why was she acting this way? Fear gripped her. She wasn't equipped to deal with loss. She needed her mother. Grace couldn't be sick. "Anything."

"Anything?"

"Yes, just agree to see the medic. I can tell something is not right."

"Deal." Her mother turned, smiling brightly. Mede froze. That was not the forlorn expression Grace had been wearing moments before. "Wait here. You are going to love what I have for you."

Mede watched as her mother straightened her shoulders and pushed the wayward strands of her hair back into the bun braided at the nape of her neck. Mede eyed her mother in shock. What had just happened? Did her sweet, innocent mother just manipulate her into agreeing to…what?

"I had this made for you." Grace lifted a gown

proudly before her. "You will be the most beautiful bride at the festival."

"I'm not going to the festival," Mede said numbly, eyeing the frilly dress. "And what is that thing? It locks like a normal dress got attacked by lacey stuff, and lost."

"Don't be silly, daughter, of course you're going. Just as I'm going to see a medic. Your dragon honor dictates that you uphold our agreement." Grace continued to smile, ignoring the comments about the dress.

"Did you just manipulate me?" Mede couldn't move. She had not seen that coming. Yes, she knew her mother wanted her to go to the festival, but she never in a million lifetimes thought Grace would fake an illness to manipulate her into going.

"Oh, daughter." Grace gave a secretive smile. "I've asked you for years to let me teach you how to be a lady. You silly dragons always think you have to do things with force. Your father is the same way, only he doesn't realize when I gently push him in a direction for his own good. Had I not intervened, your name would have been Thor."

"Ah." The sound came out strangely from her throat. "You planned this."

"No, I beat you with your own stubbornness. I'm actually surprised it took you this long to catch on. Did you really think it was your idea to have your room so clean as a child?"

"I didn't want to be eaten by yorkins who'd be attracted to the smell of…" Mede frowned. "Wait a moment, yorkins never come into this part of the mountains."

Grace wiggled the dress in the air. "Try this on."

Mede didn't move to take the garment, instead eyeing it as if it would strike out and bite her like a poisonous givre from the marshes. "So do you manipulate father often?"

"I persuade," Grace corrected. "When you're married you'll understand. Men like to be men. Let them. Let them think what you want them to do is their idea. Stop trying so hard to be a man, Medellyn. You act as if males are the only ones with natural tools at their disposal. Men need women to help them. They don't always admit it, especially these alpha dragon types, but in many ways a woman's gifts are so much more powerful than brute strength."

Mede was speechless.

"Close your mouth, dear," Grace said.

Mede did. The words stunted with disbelief, she muttered, "You had that dress sewn for me. You knew you would get me to go to the festival."

"Of course I had the dress made. A lady always

plans ahead. Now try it on for me." Grace pressed the garment against her daughter's chest forcing Mede to hold on to it. Lowering her tone, she added, "Or come the festival it might not fit right. You don't want to be naked in the receiving line, do you? Though that might get me grandchildren faster."

Mede gasped that her mother would even think to utter such a teasing comment. Grace started to hum happily as she moved back to arrange her little plate of biscuits, leaving her daughter to stare after her in stunned silence.

"Is going naked still an option?" Mede frowned as she stood in the bridal gown feeling like she was being strangled by material. The corset bodice was fitted to her waist so tight she could barely breathe and she was pretty sure her breasts had never been pushed so high in her life. Her mother had cinched her in, pulling strings along her back as if Mede might otherwise escape the horrendous thing and run away. Luckily the dress hid her scar before her mother could see it, though the tight press of the corset did cause it to ache. "Tell the truth. This is really some kind of prisoner device."

The skirt stirred around her legs as she moved —silk fabric overlaid with more lace. So much lace. It would be impossible to run without tripping.

"I wore a corset when I married your father," Grace said. "It is good luck to wear something old fashioned."

"I think breathing is pretty lucky. How about we do that?" Mede panted.

"You'll get used to it," her mother said, unconcerned. "It will keep you from running away."

Her mother knew her so well.

"And this," Grace said, holding up white gauze, "is your veil."

Grace slipped a bracelet of silk over Mede's wrist. A long piece of gauze was attached to it. She first ran the strip of flimsy material behind Mede's back before attaching a second bracelet to the other wrist. "Beautiful."

Mede tried to pull her hands forward only to discover the wrist veil limited her movements significantly. She pulled one hand forward which forced the other hand behind her back.

"Get me out of this," Mede said, trying to wiggle free.

"Is someone outside?" her mother questioned.

"What?" Mede turned, stunned to watch her mother leave her. "No, come back. Untie me!"

The sound of muffled voices caught her attention. Mede reached behind her back, breathing hard as she tried to figure out how to loosen the corset to escape the bridal gown. The effort made her lightheaded and she swayed.

"Prince Llyr, welcome, do come in and sit down." Grace's voice carried from the other room. "I'm sorry, but my husband is with the herd. One of the ceffyls is expecting a baby."

Mede stiffened. What was the prince doing here? Her arm instantly tingled, but she wasn't sure if it was the memory of his touch, or the lack of blood flow in her body. She pulled at her waist and stomach, trying to loosen the material. Her lungs began to burn. Tiny prickling sensations made her legs weak as she stumbled to the door.

"Can't...breathe," she whispered. "Can't..."

CHAPTER 6

Llyr tried not to look around too eagerly at the small mountain home. Whereas in his home he was surrounded by carved stone, this house was built of wood. The textured grains of the walls were still evident in the smoothed planks. It was immaculately cleaned and decorated. Though the entire house would easily fit into his wing of the palace, this place felt more welcoming than his did.

Tiny bowls filled with dried flowers were evenly spaced along the length of a short-legged, long table next to a couch. Closing his eyes briefly, he expected to detect their decay. Instead, he smelled a heady perfume mix that seemed to exude from the dried petals. A small fireplace had been stacked with wood, ready to light, though the days had been warm. Floral-print material covered the window. It matched the pattern on the couch. By the softer hues, he guessed the lady of the house did the decorating. Axell didn't really seem like the house type. Whenever Llyr met Mede's father, he smelled of the outdoors—a not unpleasant combination of ceffyl and fresh mountain air.

Since officially meeting Mede at the campsite, he had made it his business to learn everything he could about her family, in hopes of initiating conversation when he saw her next. Her father was known to him. As the main ceffyl breeder on the planet, Axell was well respected and liked. His gruff manners did not faze the Draig in the least. Her mother, however, had a charitable reputation. Most of the stories about her consisted of how she brought food to the sick and helped new mothers to clean their homes so that they may rest after labor. Actually, he'd thought maybe the talk of her good deeds was inflated, until today, when he'd met her and looked upon her face. There was virtuousness in her, the kind of decency that reflected through the eyes from the spirit. It couldn't be faked. When he looked at Lady Grace, he found himself literally wanting to be a better person.

And then there was Grace's daughter. Mede was a strange mix of her beautiful mother and her fierce dragon father. Even now the nerves in his fingers remembered how she felt against them—

and that had only been her arm. He balled his fist tightly together, trying to erase the feeling so he could concentrate.

Lady Grace smiled courteously at him, and waited for him to speak. He had the impression she'd wait as long as it took, without rudely pointing out that he merely gawked at her home after arriving there uninvited.

Llyr walked toward the display of old weapons on the wall. "These are very impressive."

"My husband's family—" Grace began.

"Can't breathe."

Llyr turned in surprise just in time to catch Mede as she fell toward him. Her limp body draped into his arms. Without thought, he lifted her against him. Her head rolled to rest on his shoulder. Shallow breaths hit the side of his neck, so light that he heard more than felt them. The sudden shock of holding her almost weakened his knees, and he stiffened his legs so as not to fall over.

"Oh," Grace gasped. She waved that Llyr should put Mede on the couch. He obeyed the lady's silent bidding. Even as he sat, he didn't want to release his hold.

"Tomos, a medical unit, quick," Llyr called to his man waiting outside, knowing that Tomos would hear him with his keen senses.

"Keep her upright," Grace directed.

Llyr held Mede tighter at the command, pulling her to his chest. He wasn't sure he could let her go. His fingers kneaded against her skin. The scent of her hair filled him and he breathed deeply, while trying not to have an inappropriate reaction to her nearness. He'd dreamed of holding her, but never did he think this moment would come so soon.

Grace jerked at Mede's back, loosening the laces of her bodice. As the material gave way, Mede gasped almost instantly for breath. She drew her head up.

"I always wore it that tight," Grace said. "You'll get used to it."

Mede blinked several times before flinching. "Ow." Her right arm was trapped awkwardly at her side. She leaned left. He didn't let her go as she straightened the limb. "What…"

Mede's gray gaze found his. At first, he thought her eyes were completely monochromatic, but up close he could see the thin threads of violet in them. For a long, wonderful moment, she didn't fight him. Instead, she merely looked at him, as if content to be held.

"I have the medical unit," Tomos said, hurrying in the door. His dark brown eyes were hidden by his even darker hair as it fell forward over his face. It was clear the man had rushed to produce the unit from Llyr's pack. Tomos had a good heart, and often accompanied the prince when he came to the mountains—mainly because he was a son of miners and had been born in Mining Village. He went back as often as he could to visit his parents.

Mede stiffened at the sound and pushed her arms against Llyr's chest. She eyed the dormant crystal at his neck. The softness left her as she forced him to release his hold. Well, in truth, he could have probably kept her against him with brute force, but he didn't think that would make the best impression on Mede or her mother.

"What happened?" Mede's gaze met her mother's.

Tomos slowly stepped closer to the couch. "Do you need this?"

"Yes," Llyr said.

"No," Mede answered at the same time.

"Yes," Llyr said again, the word coming out forcefully so that Tomos would know it was an order. He rarely used his position to get his way, but this was a special case. Mede's eyes challenged him. Grace motioned that Tomos should proceed.

Tomos eyed the unit for a moment. He was a miner who had yet to try for a wife, and was not used to medically examining women. The fact that Mede was perhaps one of the first unmated women he'd ever come across would make his situation worse. He glanced at his crystal, seeming to relax a tiny degree when it didn't glow.

"Tomos," Llyr insisted, attempting to give the man permission with the sound of his voice, and thus the encouragement he clearly needed to proceed.

Confused, Tomos started to reach forward with the medical unit only to pull his hand back.

"Perhaps I should?" Grace offered.

Tomos practically thrust the unit at the lady in relief, and retreated outside to give them privacy. Llyr chuckled. Whoever was fated for Tomos would have to be strong willed. He doubted the man would make the first move, even if the gods themselves came down and told him who to marry.

"I'm fine," Mede insisted. Her tone was even but she glared at him from the opposite end of the couch. He wondered if the pleasantness of her voice was for her mother's benefit.

Now that distance was between them, Llyr was able to look at her gown. The tight bodice of the wedding dress defined her waist and hips, in a way the long tunic shirt she wore the night of her initiation into the brotherhood, had not. It also pushed up her breasts like two very tempting offerings. Llyr wasn't sure what he wanted to do more—grab them, or jealously hide them from the view of others.

Wait, no, that was a lie. He definitely wanted to grab them more than hide them. They looked so soft.

Grace ran the medical unit over her daughter's chest and head. The motion broke his fixated gaze. Llyr realized he'd been staring at Mede's breasts like a fool. He tried to avert his eyes from the women, but it didn't work. So as a compromise, he looked at Mede's face.

"It says your heart is racing a little fast." Grace glanced at Mede and then the prince. "And your temperature is higher than normal."

Mede snatched the device from her mother. "Of course it is. You tried to strangle me with a wedding gown. I think it's a sign from the gods not to go to the festival."

Llyr tensed and had to keep himself from interrupting.

"Nice try. You're going. I have your word." Then, grinning, Grace took the unit from her daughter and began scanning herself. When she finished, she turned the screen so Mede could see. "All clear."

"If I have to go to the festival, then you have to go see a medic. That was the deal, not to simply use a medical unit. I believe the closest medic lives at the base of the mountains near the palace, mother."

Grace actually paled. "Let me give this back to Tomos."

"Your mother needs medical attention? I will send Tomos to the palace at once," Llyr said, moving to stand.

Mede grabbed his wrist. "Don't you dare. If she wants me to suffer by trying to find a life mate, she can suffer by riding a ceffyl. She hates those things."

"But your father—"

"Right? And everyone says the gods are so good at making matches. Yet they paired the ceffyl breeder and the noblewoman who gets nervous around large animals. That's why you don't see any herds near the house most of the time. If you ask me, the gods are well liquored when they're pairing us up." Mede let go of him. He wished she wouldn't. Her touch sent shockwaves over him. How could she not feel it too? How could he not affect her as fiercely as she affected him? Even now she looked like she wanted to hit him, when all he could do was think about kissing her.

MEDE WANTED nothing more than to claw the eyes out of Llyr's head. Gods' bones those eyes were dangerous. When he looked at her he made her weak inside. She hated to feel weak. And when he'd held her…oh, when he held her. She took a deep breath, still feeling every inch of his body as if it had never left hers.

Each nerve tingled violently. Her heart raced. And, yes, even her temperature was too hot. She'd almost sarcastically thanked her mother for pointing that embarrassing fact out. As if fainting wasn't bad enough.

Again she looked at Llyr's necklace. Nothing. No glow. No destiny standing right in front of her. Just a man—a sexy, aggravatingly perfect dragon man.

Mede stood and moved toward the back rooms so she could take off the ridiculous dress. She tried to think of something clever to say, but nothing came to mind so she stayed quiet and endeavored not to look like she was running away from the prince's presence.

Once alone, she struggled to get out of the corset. After she'd finally managed to wiggle it down her hips and off her legs, she launched it at the wall. It made a *thwap* sound before falling on the floor. Almost defiantly, she took several deep breaths. How was a woman supposed to run or fight in that horrific torture device? Mede could barely manage to walk across the house in it.

Going to her trunk, she found herself grabbing

a pretty tunic dress instead of her normal pants and shirt. Her mother would be so happy if she wore it. Even as she put the dress back and grabbed a plain shirt instead, she knew she was being childish. She slipped on her pants and boots before heading back out to the living area.

Grace smiled at her. "Prince Llyr is on his way to speak to your father."

Mede nodded and avoided looking at the prince directly. "He's not here. Try the north valleys."

"So your mother told me," Llyr said.

Did his voice have to be all low and smooth? She trembled.

"Nice of you to come by," Mede lied. If she never saw him again, never felt all shivery and weak from his touch, it would be too soon.

"Mede," Grace said firmly. A smile remained on her pleasant features despite the warning in her tone. Undoubtedly, Grace wanted Mede to invite him to dinner, which would turn into twelve unbearably slow courses—delicious courses, but slow. "As I have to prepare to go to the palace to see a medic, you will need to escort Prince Llyr to where your father is in the western field."

Mede's eyes rounded. "But—"

"You should be able to track him quite easily," Grace said.

"But…" Mede's mind raced for a way out. She stepped closer to her mother and lowered her voice, though she knew Llyr could still hear her if he wanted to. He was standing only a few feet away. "Propriety. You always say women should never go with men unescorted."

Grace actually laughed as if Mede had told a very humorous joke. "On my Victorian home world with *human* males. Since when do you recognize propriety?"

Mede knew telling her mother she'd been camping had been a mistake.

"What are you worried about?" Grace whispered. "He's Draig and his crystal is dormant. Take the prince to see your father."

Mede looked at the prince, silently begging him to let her out of it.

"Your presence will be a welcome addition to our traveling party," Llyr said.

Curse him.

"We'll wait for you to gather whatever belongings you need for the trip," he added.

"Why? Are you unable to run? The western fields are not that far," she challenged. "I can run there and back by tonight if we don't stop."

"We're worried about a couple of the ceffyls. We thought it best to bring them to your father, instead of summoning him to the palace away from the herd. They're traveling slowly." Llyr did not rise to her baiting.

"My father is not going to be happy with that," she mumbled, going to pack a bag. Mede hoped it wouldn't be more than one night—though how she was going to make it through one night in the same campsite as Llyr, she wasn't sure.

CHAPTER 7

Var Palace, Attor's Bedchamber

"What do you mean you don't know where she is?" Attor demanded, glaring at the guard. "How hard is it to find one female dragon?"

He paced his bedchamber in frustration. It was as if Mede had disappeared. Where were they keeping her? He'd sent his best scouts into Draig territory to find her. He should have her in front of him by now.

"We've been watching the skies, but we haven't seen her," the guard, Novem, defended.

"The skies?" Attor tried to take a deep breath to calm his outrage. If he wasn't so disappointed, he would have laughed at the man. Instead, he grabbed the nearest object—a bronzed rendition of the Var royal crest—and flung it at Novem's head.

91

"She can't fly, you *hurtyn*! Those are children's stories."

The guard dodged the crest and looked as if he wanted to escape.

"Why are you staring at me?" Attor yelled. "Go back. Find her. Search the mountains this time."

Novem nodded once and quickly backed out of the room. Attor grabbed a decorative pot and threw it. The antique shattered but it didn't make him feel better. The memory of the kiss haunted him. He wanted Lady Mede. He wanted to dominate her, make her his queen. Seeing her, touching her, had made his path very clear. She understood him. She could love him. He'd seen the sympathy in her eyes when she'd talked of the prince. Why hadn't he told her he was the prince?

Why hadn't he finished his seduction in the forest that night?

Attor looked down the length of his body to his erection. He felt out of control. Where was Myrddin with his nef? He needed to temper back his desires, control them.

Almost angrily he turned to the footsteps entering his room. A maid carried a bucket of hot water and a satchel of cleaning supplies. She froze when she saw him.

"I-I was about to clean the hall. Th-th-the

guard said to…" She gestured toward the broken pot and made a cleaning gesture.

"Leave it," Attor commanded. Then, eyeing her waist, he added, "Take off that gown and get in the bed." Her blonde hair and rounded figure were not what he wanted, though they were very pretty to look at.

"I'm married," she whispered in shock.

"Then send me someone who isn't!" Attor yelled.

The woman ran from the room, leaving her bucket behind. Attor grabbed another antique, a statue of a shifting cat, and threw it. The metal clanged, bouncing across the floor but not breaking.

The walls of the palace were closing in on him. He hated his life, hated his weak father and dead mother. That rage fueled him. Ever since he'd decided to take Mede as his wife, life without her had become unbearable. Fucking brought some relief, but it was always temporary.

Where was that maid? How dare she use marriage as an excuse not to obey him? What was taking her so long? He should have made her get on her knees for him, married or not. She was a servant. It was her job to see to his needs—all of them.

Attor threw another statue, aiming in the direction where its metal twin had landed. The clanking noise still did nothing to ease his anger.

"Just bring me my bride," he whispered through gritted teeth. "I want my bride."

"WHY ARE you so averse to marriage? Your parents seem very well suited to each other." Llyr watched Mede carefully as she walked next to one of the sick ceffyls.

"This ceffyl ate solarflowers," Mede answered. The large animal walked slowly with its center horn pointed more forward than up as its head drooped. It stayed close to Mede as if the creature remembered her from its ceffylhood. Chances were it did. The creature opened its mouth and slithered a long tongue against Mede's arm. The action was slow and the reptilian eyes had a glassy sheen. "And then she was given her normal food. That's what's wrong with her. They can't eat solarflowers and normal food close together. It's toxic to them."

"That doesn't answer my question. Why do you dislike the idea of marriage?"

"You should really take better care of the animals in your charge." Mede kept walking, not looking at him. The cool mountain breeze gave an odd contrast to the heat of midday. Seeing the orb of the blue sun reminded him of how rare Mede's birth was. The temperatures on the planet were always warm, though it could get chilly in the mountains. The blue radiation genetically altered the men so they produced mostly sons.

"So you're not going to answer my question?"

"How hard is it to make sure there are no solarflowers near their grazing land?" she asked.

Llyr chuckled. "Fine. You don't want to answer."

Mede glanced over her shoulder to where Tomos followed behind them. He was too far back to listen easily. "Every male during my training tried to claim me as a bride. My mother wants me to have a thousand children. My father wants anything that will please my mother. I want to be treated like an equal and not a brood mare."

"*Only* a thousand?" Llyr drawled wryly.

Mede turned a shocked look toward him and then started to laugh. "Yes, only a thousand."

"So your mother wants to be a grandmother and boys had crushes on you when you were a child, so naturally you don't want to marry just to be contrary?"

Mede grimaced. "Don't say it like that. It makes it sound ridiculous."

"Well…"

She arched a brow. "I won't apologize for being

me and wanting what I want—not to a commoner, not to a Var, not to the Prince of all the Draig, not to the King of the Accursed Universe. So you smile your handsome little smile and think whatever you want, but insult my life choices again and that's one battle you'll lose to a girl."

Llyr tried to look properly chastised.

"And you're baiting me, aren't you?" she asked in exasperation.

Llyr couldn't maintain innocence and started to laugh. "You think my smile is handsome?"

"I think you, prince, are teasing me." Mede reached her hand to pet the ceffyl as they walked. Her long, delicate fingers glanced over the center of the animal's face. "I'm just not sure why."

"Maybe I like you," Llyr admitted. It was only a fraction of the truth. When he looked at her, he felt as if he'd found himself. When she touched him, his skin lit on fire and a shockwave rocked him to the very core. He thought of her more than he thought of himself. He wanted desperately to win her, not because the crystal glowing in his pocket told him they were fated but because she chose him. He wanted her to choose him. As Draig, they spent their whole lives being told that the gods knew what was best when it came to the heart and would reward those who lived honorably and did their duty.

This practice contradicted independent dragons like Mede who wouldn't appreciate being told what to do.

"I was very excited when I heard your father had contracted Galaxy Brides Corporation for a steady shipment of brides who would agree to marry strangers. Trading rocks for brides is genius." She sighed dramatically. "I had hoped it would distract the men with new blood, but I quickly discovered that it still didn't stop men from proposing to me."

Mede was a strange and complicated woman. He could tell as much within five seconds of meeting her. Actually, he'd concluded as much before he'd even officially met her. She'd defied gods and tradition by crushing her own crystal—and she didn't appear to regret it.

No, a woman like Mede wouldn't want his crystal telling her what to do. She'd need to discover her future for herself. Just because the crystal glowed, it didn't mean the bride had to say yes.

Llyr needed her to say yes.

"Why are you looking at me like that?" she asked.

"You have dirt on your nose," he answered.

Mede wiped at her face. Llyr laughed.

Realizing he again teased, she made a small

playful noise of discontent and turned her attention to the path in front of them once more.

Draig Northern Mountains, Western Fields

Mede absently patted the sick beast as she walked, trying to give the ceffyl some comfort. Her father had taught her a lot about the herds, especially after he'd found out what she'd done to her crystal. Though he never really said anything directly to her, she had the feeling he wanted her to have a skill in case she never married. Taking care of the herds was an honorable job, one that would ensure her future and Axell's legacy—at least for one more generation.

The western fields were easy to find. They consisted of a series of connected valleys that led between jagged cliffs. The rocky walls provided safety and shade for the herds. Finding which nook of those valleys her father was holed up in proved to be more difficult. Instead, she watched the ceffyls for signs that others were nearby.

Llyr was pleasant company. She couldn't fault him for his charm and likeability, but she still found herself tense from his nearness. Coming to consciousness in his arms after being strangled by a wedding gown had been a surreal experience.

Those green eyes of his had pierced into her, until confusion and desire had locked her muscles and made resistance impossible. Though the moment had been brief by any real standard, it felt like it had lasted an eternity in her mind.

Part of her said to run.

Part of her said to kiss him.

The majority of her told the rest of her, to keep quiet and get control of her emotions.

Mede couldn't explain the thread that filtered out of her toward him. She found herself looking at his neck, to the dormant stone. Everything in her culture told her they were not meant to be together. From his neck, her gaze moved down to his chest. When he walked, the tunic molded to his muscles. She remembered the press of his stomach to hers when he'd held her on the couch. There were plenty of well-shaped men on her planet, but for some reason she found herself looking at Llyr with renewed sight. Her steps faltered and she fell a few paces behind him. The breeze blew his shirt against his spine, burrowing into the indent cutting down his back.

Tingling erupted in her lower stomach. Mede did not want to be married. She clung to that fact. As everything else inside her turned to turmoil, she had to go with logic.

"My lady?" Llyr questioned.

Mede realized she'd stopped walking. Instead of admitting she'd been staring at his backside, she pointed to the distance. "My father likes to camp near that cave. If he's not there, we can track him from there."

Llyr lifted his hand and motioned back to Tomos before changing directions to walk toward the cave.

Mede closed her eyes and took a deep breath. The mountain air was sweet in the valleys. The blend of grasses and tiny blue flowers mixed with the almost acidic smell of porous black rocks that littered the ground, like forgotten pieces of the past.

"I don't think I've ever been to this part of our territory before," Llyr said.

"Not many people come here," Mede answered. "There is nothing here but grazing land for the ceffyls. It's protected territory. Nothing to hunt. No reason to come."

Llyr reached down and picked up a black rock. He bounced it in his hand. "I haven't seen aphanitic stones like this either?"

"Aphanitic?" She frowned.

"See the fine grains? It happens when rocks cool fast from high temperatures." He ran his finger down the center of the rock.

She watched the touch, captivated by his fingertip. "You like rocks?"

"I like reading," he admitted. Llyr dropped his hand but held the rock, as if he'd keep it. "You said earlier that we trade rocks for brides. We actually trade ore, not simply rocks. Ore is a big part of our planetary economy, so I read about it. Then I read about other rocks and minerals. Then I read about making ore into fuel. Then I read about the engines that use the fuel."

Mede reached her hand out for the rock. He glanced at her questioningly before handing it over.

"You should have read about our laws." She dropped the rock on the ground. "This land is protected, which means removing stones is forbidden."

"Only if I'm caught." Llyr took a bold step closer. His gaze dipped to her lips. "You won't tell on me, will you?"

"What would be the point?" She arched a brow. It was hard to act nonchalant when he was close. She imagined she could feel the heat from his body. Her eyes went to his chest, to the cracked crystal. Unsure as to why, she lightly touched the cool stone. There was more hum between their un-touching bodies than in the crystal against her fingers. "I have a feeling you would not be imprisoned for the offence."

"Are you saying I would use my position to break the law?" He reached his hand to cover hers. Her nerves jumped to life.

"You might not want to do that with her father watching you," Tomos said casually as he walked past. "He looks irritated. And really tough."

Mede jerked her hand away with a gasp. She spun around to see her father standing near a small cave entrance.

Axell's arms were crossed over his thick chest. She could see how someone would think her father was intimidating. He rarely smiled and had a dry wit that left others pondering his true meaning. Mede smiled at him and rushed forward. Mostly, she hurried away from Llyr. She needed to put distance between them.

"A few of the palace ceffyls appear to have gotten into solarflowers," Mede said. She paused to kiss his cheek. "Prince Llyr brought them up for you to look at. He needed a guide to find you so mother sent me."

"Did they let them eat afterwards?" Axell asked. He placed his hand lovingly on his daughters shoulder and nodded once in greeting.

"I believe so," Mede answered. Solarflowers needed to be starved out of the creatures so they didn't become ill from the mild toxins released when they combined with other foods in the digestive process. The real problem was that ceffyls could find a single solarflower in an acre of field, like a marsh farmer could sniff out a liquor still in the shadowed marshes. "They show classic symptoms."

"I'll check them." Her father sighed loudly. "See to the newborn for me."

"Live?" she asked.

"Yes, early this morning. He's a sickly little thing." Her father motioned that she should go inside the cave. "It's fortunate you came. The more he bonds to others, the better chance he'll have at surviving."

She entered the cave and found a ceffyl baby bundled in her father's bedroll. The cave was small with smoothed stone floors and ledges. Even with a small fire, the light was dim, but she could see easily. The baby ceffyl would do better in the cooler temperature and darker environment.

The creature's tiny face poked out of a small opening in the bedding. Its long tongue hung from its mouth and trembled with each breath. Mede sat on the dirt floor and moved the solid bundle onto her lap. She scratched the soft nub on the animal's head where a horn would later grow. It made a happy gurgling noise and stretched stubby legs against the bedding.

"There's a little beast," she whispered softly. "Open your eyes and connect."

The creature slowly obeyed her gentle prodding. Milky brown eyes found hers.

"Good little beast."

LLYR LISTENED to Mede's affectionate voice as she spoke to the ceffyl. Raw emotion made an unsteady path over his body. It became impossible to move. The tenderness brought forth an intense longing. His hand automatically moved beneath his tunic to reach into his pocket. The crystal was warm and he knew it glowed. The hum of energy coming from it radiated over him. His palm itched, the power of it almost burning his skin.

"It would have been better if you starved them until the flowers were digested. At least three days."

Llyr gave a little jolt of surprise and let go of the stone in his pocket as he turned to face Mede's father. He'd always respected Axell and didn't mind his gruff nature. "I didn't bring her flowers."

Axell glanced into the cave where his daughter was and then back at the prince.

"Oh, the solarflowers," Llyr quickly amended, forcing his brain to focus. "I wasn't sure the ceffyls had gotten into any. I have the stable boys constantly on the lookout for them, but they grow like weeds by the palace."

"Tell me, how is it no one there recognizes solarflower sickness in the ceffyls? As you said, they grow like weeds." Axell studied him.

Llyr couldn't meet the man's perceptive gaze.

"Why have you really come to speak to me?" Axell asked. "I've heard rumors that the Var have been scented coming over the borders. I assumed it was like our young ones running over their borders for a bit of rebellion."

Llyr looked back at the cave, listening for Mede. He thought of the night he'd been introduced to her.

"Is it more than that?" The man frowned. "If you've come to ask me for more ceffyl stock, I cannot rush the process. I won't overbreed my herd."

Inside the cave, Mede talked gently to the animal like it was her own baby.

"What is Mede doing in there?" Llyr asked.

Axell laughed. "Ah, so you didn't come for me. At least tell me you didn't feed the solarflowers to the animals on purpose."

Llyr chuckled, knowing the man was joking with him. Axell knew he'd never hurt an animal. He gave a sheepish look at the ground.

"She's helping the animal bond," Axell said.

"They will be more social in life if they connect to people when they're newborn, but it has to be a calm setting." The man studied him. "Mede has a soft spot for animals. You should go in and offer to help. You can leave the sick animals with me. I'll make sure they purge the flowers."

Llyr smiled, grateful for the advice. "And Tomos will help you with the ceffyls before we leave for Mining Village. That's our next stop. He has family there. Lady Grace also asked that we bring you food."

"My wife undoubtedly sent enough to feed the whole Draig army. You must join me for a meal before you leave."

Llyr nodded. "Our pleasure."

"Thank you. I would like to spend some time with my daughter but in this case..." Axell glanced toward the cave entrance. "Tell Mede you need a guide out of the valley. But act like a prince or—"

"You'll come after me like any father would?"

"No." Axell shook his head in denial and placed his hand on Llyr's shoulder. "My daughter will trap you in the mines and leave you where no one can find you. That dragon has a temper."

Llyr gave a nervous laugh.

"And you might want to wrap that stone in your pocket in some darker material. When you stand in the shadows I can see it glowing through your tunic."

Llyr needlessly glanced down. "I can explain."

"No need. I've met my daughter." Axell's brusque laugh was low as he went to a pack near the cave entrance. He reached in and took out a square piece of cloth before handing it to Llyr. "I wish you luck, prince. You'll need it."

Llyr watched the man as he walked toward the sick ceffyls. He wrapped his crystal in the cloth before putting it back in his pocket. A small wave of guilt came over him, but he couldn't bring himself to show her yet. He wanted her to know as innately as he did that they were destined to be together.

It was easy to discover where Mede was in the cave. Following the subtle glow of firelight, he found her sitting on the floor with the baby animal in her lap. A glance down his side ensured the glow was hidden from her.

"There's my sweet love. I don't know how I missed it before now," she said.

Llyr's entire being stiffened at her soft words.

"It all makes perfect sense, doesn't it?" she continued.

His heartbeat quickened and he fumbled eagerly for his pocket to show her their destiny. This was it. She would see. She did see.

"Get out." Mede's tone lowered slightly. "Your restlessness is breaking my connection."

Llyr realized her words had not been for him. He gave a short laugh at himself for acting like a hapless fool.

"There's the spot," she continued speaking to the animal.

"Will you show me how it's done?" Llyr asked.

Mede nodded without looking at him. The firelight caressed her skin with an orange hue. He moved closer. She held the ceffyl baby on her crossed legs while she stared into its eyes. Llyr sat next to her, purposefully letting their legs touch.

"They can't see very well at this age, so you need to make sure your face is close." Mede kept her voice soft and gentle. "It doesn't matter what you say as much as the way you say it. And this one likes it when you rub his horn nob like this." Mede glided her finger back and forth over the baby's head. "How did I miss that spot before? Yeah, you like that don't you. Should we let the prince try?"

The animal slithered its tongue. The long, thin length licked at Mede's arms. She finally broke eye contact and smiled. "You see that. It worked. He likes me."

"What's not to like?" Llyr reached to touch Mede's face. She misinterpreted the gesture and stuck the animal in his arms.

"When he licks you, you're bonded for life." Mede patted his arm and stood.

"You're not staying?" He began to stand but the creature stirred and made a noise of protest.

"It works better if you're alone." She left the cave.

Llyr sighed. Then looking at the little beast, he said, "You'll have to teach me your secret. You're with her for two seconds and already have her bonded to you."

The animal made a strange grunting noise and thumped his feet against Llyr's chest.

Llyr arched a brow and gave a short laugh. "Fine." He rubbed the creature's head as he'd seen Mede do. Instantly the animal calmed. "Try to keep your secret, ceffyl."

THERE WAS much to be said about late afternoons in the valley. They reminded Mede of childhood, of being made to run a mile to touch a jagged rock and back again, as her father timed her speed. Only later did she realize he sent her away so he could work without her leaning over his shoulder to watch, and incessantly ask questions.

Campfire light glowed softly in a dirt clearing. The fire was more for warmth than light. Mede inhaled a deep breath of fresh air. The cooling grasses gave off the subtle smell of sweet vanilla. It would only linger for about an hour before fading. In all her running around the wilderness, she'd never found a similar scent anywhere else on the planet.

"He likes you," Axell stated, laughing.

Mede looked at her father and then followed his gaze to where Llyr held the baby ceffyl. Llyr moved as if to set the animal down. The creature protested by kicking his feet. The prince gave in and adjusted it in his arms. The baby instantly settled.

Mede's laughter joined her father's. Axell reached into the food satchel her mother had sent and handed her a cloth bundle. The shape and weight was familiar to her and she smiled in anticipation before even unwrapping it. As she peeled back a corner to reveal the flaky meat-filled pastry, she stopped mid-bite to see Llyr staring at her. He had a strange look on his face, one she couldn't decipher.

She closed her mouth without taking a bite, looked down at her food, and then extended her hand toward him so he could eat without putting the animal down. The action forced her to lean forward. He parted his lips slowly, but he didn't lower his eyes. She trembled nervously as she watched the food slip past his lips.

"Here," Axell said with a small clearing of his throat. "Let me take the little one from you, or he'll start thinking you're his mother. I believe Tomos should be done repacking his supplies. I'll have him bond to this little beast. He'll be one of the most social creatures I've raised in a long time." He took the protesting ceffyl from the prince and carried it away from the campfire, leaving them alone.

Mede quickly looked away from Llyr. What was she doing? Her heart raced and her head felt as if she'd spun in circles and had yet to stop twirling. She found herself wondering if his broken crystal had somehow stopped working correctly because she felt a pull toward Llyr. It was fierce and hot, and she suspected if she didn't put distance between them soon something would come of it.

Fate was pretty clear. They were not meant to be together as man and wife. But what if they were meant to be together as something else? Mede knew the men of the planet sometimes found physical pleasure with offworld unmated women. Onworld she was the only unmated female and that wasn't an option.

But, what if?

She didn't meet Llyr's gaze as she held out the meat pastry he'd taken a bite out of. His finger brushed hers as he took it from her. The shock of the brief contact worked its way up her arm.

Stay cr run?

Her body begged her to stay. To touch him just one more time. Two more times. Three…

Her mind yelled to run. This was exactly the thing she'd never wanted to feel. She'd just joined the Dead Dragons, proven herself one of the elite.

She was a dragon-shifter first. Always a dragon. Not a woman. Not like her mother. She was fierce and independent. She had a warrior's soul. She...

She couldn't quit looking at his lips, couldn't erase the tingling in her fingers where they'd made contact. The war inside her made her want to cry out. His eyes picked up a gleam from the firelight. The magnetic pull became worse. It was as if the gods played tricks with her.

Curse the gods.

Curse the prince.

Curse her body's betrayal of her mind.

"I'm sure Tomos would like to go to the village to see his family soon. It's not a long journey," Mede said in an effort to dismiss the prince from the campsite. Being alone with Llyr made it very hard for her to maintain her composure.

"I thought you'd like to spend time with your father before we left," Llyr answered, not looking like he was going to move anytime soon.

"I did plan on staying with my father to help him while you went to Mining Village," she said.

"Your father insisted you show us out of the valley." His charming smile stayed intact. She wondered if he could help the look. Being born the future king probably gave him the confidence that radiated from every look and gesture. Gods' bones, that look was alluring.

"How is it our prince can't navigate himself out of a valley?" Mede asked.

"Perhaps I want the company," he said.

"Perhaps I had important plans you're interrupting," she answered.

"Tomos is going to abandon me for his family, and I don't want to impose upon them. I thought about exploring the mines." Llyr gave a meaningful look around. "Surely a fellow Dead Dragon wouldn't be averse to some adventure."

At the mention of the mines, she sat a little straighter in excitement. "I haven't been in the mines. They're dangerous and restricted to the miners."

"I'll tell you a secret," he whispered, leaning in to her. She automatically moved closer to hear it. "I'm a member of the ruling family. I can pretty much go anywhere I want with anyone I want."

His breath whispered over her cheek. The light caress was like fire to her skin. She found herself nodding.

"Wonderful." Llyr kept his voice low. "I will enjoy finding trouble with you."

"I put the ceffyl with Tomos to bond," Axell announced. Mede gasped and drew away from Llyr. Her father stood next to the fire, studying them.

Mede blinked, trying to regain her senses from

the fog that had been settling over her. She opened her mouth to babble out an excuse for her behavior, but didn't get the chance to speak.

"Your daughter has agreed to show me the fastest route to Mining Village," Llyr said.

"Mede has a good sense of direction," her father said. The words were low and even, but his pride in his daughter was evident in the way he let a small smile curl the side of his mouth.

"Unless you need me here?" Mede prompted. She wasn't sure which answer she hoped for.

"I would love your company, but no. There is nothing to be done here but watch the newborn." Axell took a seat and helped himself to a meat pastry.

"Your wife is amazing with food," Llyr said.

Axell nodded. He gave a little sigh, as if he missed his mate. "She is the perfect wife—sweet, giving, charitable, loving. I am truly a man blessed by the gods."

Mede hid her frown. Her father pretty much listed every trait Mede did not inherit.

"Did she teach you how to cook?" Llyr asked Mede.

Axell laughed, hard, and began hitting his palm against his knee. "The only thing Mede ever cooked was biscuits, and those she made as hard as rocks so she could pummel some of the local boys with them during a game of warfare."

"I didn't try to make them like rocks," Mede mumbled. "It just happened."

"By all the gods, I swear I tried to eat one and nearly broke the teeth from my head." Axell's smile widened and he laughed harder. Mede loved the sound of her father's laughter, even if her failure in the kitchen was the cause of it.

"I've made other things," Mede said in protest.

Axell wiped a tear from the corner of his eye. "Don't worry, prince, I'll share my food with you. No need to starve on your journey."

Llyr chuckled and nodded his thanks.

Mede made a sour face at both of them and reached out her hand. "May I have a pastry now?"

Axell reached into the bag and tossed the food in her direction. She caught it with one hand. "This is why I never want to marry. If I live at home I'll never have to cook or sew or do any of the boring wifely duties."

"You'd better not say that to your mother," Axell warned playfully. "She'll end your food supply faster than a dragon breathes fire."

"I like your father," Llyr said as they made their way from the campsite.

"He is a good man," she agreed.

"Are your cooking skills really that bad?" He'd be lying to himself if he didn't admit that this revelation disappointed him a little. Her mother's meat-filled concoction was one of the most delicious things he'd ever tasted.

"I won't starve, but they're not great." Mede didn't look at him. She kept her eyes forward as they reached a jutting of rocks. She pointed up. "Fastest way without ceffyls is up there."

Llyr watched her shift into dragon form and leap high into the air. Dragon, human, it didn't matter what form she took, she was exquisite. He heard Tomos' footfall coming past him. The man had also shifted so he could easily leap up the rock. Llyr's heart raced in anticipation of a run. He gave a low growl as the hard shell of his dragon overtook his body. Being shifted cooled his sexual desires somewhat but did not lessen the connection he felt toward Mede. As he landed on a rock, he saw that Mede had darted ahead, jumping from rock perch to rock perch, before finally landing on a higher pathway, and breaking out into a full run.

Not to be outdone, he eagerly followed her up the rock, to land on a narrow path behind Tomos. A wall of dirt and stone brushed past his arm, and on the other side, was a straight drop down. It wouldn't kill them, but a fall would do some damage even in their shifted state. There was just enough room to run in single file. With Tomos between them, Llyr was left with only peeks of Mede's hair and long legs as she led them through the wilderness.

MEDE GLANCED over her shoulder to see Llyr catching up to her. The narrow path opened up to a forest that would lead down to the village. The terrain became unfamiliar, but she knew the general direction. Soon she should be able to pick up sounds of miners and their families, which would help guide her the rest of the way.

She ran faster, pushing so hard her heart was bound to explode out of her chest. Dodging thick underbrush, she almost ran into a stack of fallen limbs. Mede gasped in surprise and skidded to a stop just in time to keep from impaling herself on a broken branch. Smaller limbs scratched at her, but they didn't hurt. She pushed back only to discover her hair had flown into the brush and tangled on the sharp yellow thorns. More embarrassed than anything else, she tugged at the locks to free them.

"Easy, Mede, let me," Llyr said. He breathed hard.

"Prince?" Tomos asked, stopping nearby.

"Send my greetings to your family. We will camp in the mines tonight if we are needed," Llyr called out in a gravelly voice. Mede's eyes met his. Alone? All night?

"Very good, prince," Tomos said. She heard the man continue his run.

Llyr shifted back to human form, prompting her to do the same. It would be easier to free her hair with fingertips instead of sharp talons.

"Unless you're scared of sleeping in the cave," he said, gently pulling strands of her hair free.

"Why would I be scared of a cave?"

"Trolla, the protector of the mines, doesn't take kindly to non-miners in her territory." Llyr freed the last of her locks but didn't immediately let go. He slid his fingers over the strands.

"I fear no woman," Mede said.

"You really aren't afraid of confrontation, are you?" Llyr chuckled. "Trolla is a goddess."

"No. I'm not." Mede grinned at the compliment. "But if a goddess reveals herself to us and asks us to go, I promise to leave without starting a brawl."

Llyr dropped the hair behind her shoulder and let the tip of a finger drag over the flesh of her neck. He traced a light path to where her crystal would have hung had she not destroyed it. "I have a feeling not even the gods themselves could tell you what to do, my lady."

"The name is Mede," she countered out of habit, but the words lacked their usual strength.

"Mede," he whispered. His voice was more intimate than a caress. The forest sounds became loud around them, the chirps and bleats drawing her from his spell. She shivered and pulled away, unsure of what she might do if she didn't put distance between them.

Before she could respond, a flock of red birds dove down toward the yellow thorns and plucked them from the bush. Mede made a small sound of surprise and jumped back. They were gone as fast as they'd come, disappearing into the branches.

"The town should be quiet. Come." Llyr grabbed a pack that he must have dropped when he came to help her, and then navigated a path through the forest. He walked at a brisk pace but did not resume the run. When she would push ahead of him, he held out his arm and pointed. A small home came into view. Light glowed from within and she watched a shadow pass by the window. "Take it slow. We don't want to alarm the local families."

They came to a path cut into the forest floor by

decades of foot traffic. Mining Village was nestled into a long valley lined along the north by trees and jagged cliffs, just past a ravine to the south. The flowing water provided a backdrop of sound in the valley. She focused her hearing, detecting water cascading down stone.

The town seemed a strange combination of dusty tents and newly built houses. It was evident that much care had been taken in the placement of the homes. They were clustered on a grid pattern, in a line of four houses separated by side streets. A few homes were still under construction, as if they'd started in the center of town and simply worked their way outward.

However, the surrounding tents along the edge of the village were more haphazard, situated to optimize space, and most likely, block the wind coming down from the cliffs. Tent paths converged into a main roadway leading down to the houses. The streets were dirt but the walkways up to the house were lined with cut stones.

A small group of Draig men walked toward the tents. Their tired laughter came softly and they spared Mede and Llyr a passing glance and gesture of greeting, but did not stop them. They were dressed in loose drawstring pants and tunic shirts, covered in dirt from the mines. Only their eyes and mouths were clean where they'd most likely worn goggles and respirators to work.

Llyr turned from the town toward a cliff along the ravine. Thick bushes and trees filled the landscape below, making it too hard to see how deep it really was. The water she'd heard earlier was actually a waterfall. It pounded down upon stones and echoed around the cliffs like constant thunder.

Llyr's hand on her arm drew her eyes to his. He nodded to an outcrop before shifting to jump up and then disappear over the other side. She followed him, discovering the opening to a cave behind a veil of bright green vines. He pulled them aside like a curtain to let her pass. When the vines dropped behind them, it created an insulated wall that blocked the thundering water.

Able to talk without yelling, she shifted to human form and asked, "These are our great ore mines?"

She looked along the walls of the large cavern, trying to see the Draig fortune in the thick patches of blue stone threaded with a silvery gray. Giant crystal formations blocked the path as they mimicked thick fallen trees. They glowed, the luminescence giving light to the cavern beyond. Mede ran her hand over the smooth surface, watching it turn her flesh red as it shone through her body.

Llyr hopped up and reached his hand down to

her. She ignored it, her dragon not needing help to cross. They climbed over the crystal formation. When they were once again on the cave floor, Llyr shifted back and smiled. "Yes, these are the mines."

"And is that the fuel ore? The silver?" Mede pointed to the wall where glossy silver ran alongside them as if pointing the way deeper. When she leaned close, she could just make out her reflection in it. The crunch of loose rocks gave away his position, but she didn't need to hear him to know he was behind her. She felt him. It was like an innate beacon inside her that just knew where he was in proximity to her.

"No. The ore is deeper. Come with me. I want to show you something." Llyr didn't touch her, but he didn't have to. Every brush of their bodies was burned into her flesh—his hand on her arm at the Dead Dragon campsite, his body to hers when she'd fainted into his arms, his fingers taking the food from her hand.

"Llyr?" she whispered, unsure. "What are we doing here?"

"Camping," he answered simply.

"You know that's not what I mean." She took a deep breath. He had to feel what she felt. How could he not? It was too powerful.

"Just come with me. Please." He backed away from her several steps before again turning around to lead the way deeper. The cavern narrowed and they walked until the natural cave became a manmade tunnel. At places water moved over them, detectable by the soft, echoing flow of an underground stream.

"If you're taking me to be some kind of strange sacrifice for Trolla, I'm going to be really angry," she said, trying to make a joke.

"There she is. Ask her yourself." Llyr pointed to where a terrifying female dragon had been etched into the wall. She stood tall, surrounded by tiny worshipers. Llyr looked at the carving and then Mede. "Huh, you kind of look like her minus the wings. You have her essence, I think."

Mede arched a brow. "Did you just try to compliment me?"

"You won't let me call you a lady, so I will call you a goddess," he answered, clearly teasing her.

"Careful, or Trolla will hear you."

"We're heading up there. We have to crawl, but it's worth it. Trust me." He tossed the pack up into a narrow hole before crawling in after it. Pushing it forward, he inched along.

Mede hesitated, glancing around the cave. Seeing the Trolla carving staring at her, she whispered, "We humbly ask for your protection, great one."

"Are you coming?" Llyr yelled.

Mede held her breath as she went inside the narrow space. She didn't like feeling closed in and tried to hurry. She made a weak noise as a six-legged insect nearly as big as her hand darted away from her to crawl into a hole. The rock pressed all around her and she closed her eyes. Somehow she pushed forward and only opened her eyes when she heard Llyr's pack hit the floor. He reached to pull her out of the hole to her feet.

Tiny lights danced around her like the stars on the one night of planetary darkness. The bioluminescent creatures parted to let them pass, spreading away toward the rounded walls. Llyr kicked his pack toward the center of the cave room.

"We'll camp here," he said.

"It's remarkable." Mede turned in slow circles before walking toward the wall. She tried to touch one of the lights, but the tiny creatures scattered out of her way and she couldn't even make out their true shape. "I've never seen anything like it."

"The miners call them stardust because they look like stars and live in the ground. They light up the mines and always travel in groups."

"They're glowing," Mede stated the obvious.

"Bioluminescence. They produce light to communicate with each other. At least that's what I've been told. It's said if they land on you, it's good luck." Llyr busied himself with his pack, pulling out bedrolls and laying them on the ground. "Are you hungry?"

Mede crossed to where he worked. She touched his shoulder. Llyr looked up in surprise. When she didn't move or speak, he slowly stood.

"We're not meant to be together." Mede only stated a fact, yet it caused a wave of sorrow inside her. She buried the feeling and forced herself to touch his dormant stone.

"Then walk away from me. Leave." His expression said he didn't want her to go.

She tried. Her feet wouldn't move. Her hand wouldn't leave his shoulder. "I can't."

"Then stay with me and kiss me."

"Llyr, you can see as well as I that we aren't to be married. Whatever this is cannot last. I have worked so hard for my reputation. I can't—"

"Mede, I have no wish to ruin your reputation. No one will know anything about this night that you don't tell them. I give you my word as a prince, as a dragon, and as a man. From that first moment I have wanted to kiss you but I won't force myself on you. Whatever happens will be what you want to happen." He hesitated to touch her. When she didn't pull away, his fingers glanced over her cheek. "Don't think about marriage and gods and crystals." He took off his necklace and dropped it into the open pack before resuming his caress of her face. Fingers slid down her throat to the pulse thumping in her neck. "Don't think about fate or reputation or even that world outside this magical place. What do you want? What do you feel?"

Mede couldn't hold back. She pressed her lips to his. All worry and doubt left with the touch of his mouth to hers. From that first second she'd been fighting her feelings for him. They welled inside her now, burning their way out of her stomach to fill her with fire and need. Before she could rationalize what she was doing, her fingers had gripped his shirt and she was pulling at his tunic to take it off.

Llyr broke their kiss and obligingly removed off his shirt. She dropped the material to the floor and stepped on it to return to the kiss. This time she met with naked flesh. The heat of him combined with the smooth texture of his skin mesmerized her as she explored the full length of his chest and back. Her finger met with his Dead Dragon scar and she pulled back.

"You didn't stay to see me marked," she said, her gaze dipping to his moist lips before moving back up to meet his eyes. "You left during my honor."

"How can you fault me for that? As badly as I wanted you, do you really think I could stand by and see your beautiful skin injured? I left because it was your honor. You didn't need me ruining your marking because I couldn't bear to mar this pretty body of yours."

"Then it had nothing to do with my being a female and you thinking me unworthy?"

"Unworthy? No, my lad—" Llyr quickly amended, "*Mede*. I left because if I had been forced to lift your shirt, I would have embarrassed you and greatly dishonored myself."

He slid his hand around to touch the small of her back where her scar healed beneath the tunic shirt. A small, happy laugh escaped her.

"You earned your marking. I still don't know how you managed to skin a member of the royal court." He started to lean toward her, only to pull back. "How did you manage it?"

Mede grimaced. "I don't want to tell you."

"I promise your secret will be safe with me. You didn't cheat and bring it with you, did you?"

"Of course not. I collected it that night. It's just…" She made a weak noise and then rolled her eyes heavenward. "Fine. The cat-shifter gave it to me. I wanted to fight him for it, but he refused."

"Gave it…?"

"Yes. He gave it to me. And there is no rule as to how you obtain your prize, only that you do. I was running in the forest and came across the drunken marsh farmer. I was about to take a piece of him like everyone else—which would not have been a challenge—when I heard a woman scream. Naturally, I went to help her, but then, I came across the Var. We talked. He seemed very interested in the fact that I was the female dragon. I told him I needed cat-shifter fur and he let me have his." Almost defensively, she added, "Negotiation takes more skill than brute force."

"Just like that? You asked and he gave it to you freely?"

"Well, he…" Mede's voice trailed off into a mumble.

"What?"

"He kissed me, all right!" Mede took a few steps back. His hand slid from her body. "I swear I didn't know it was coming, and it was over before I could even stick my knife in his gut. I think he was just curious about me because I'm the dragon female— just like all you men are curious about me. I'm just some prize to be had, a rare special gem to be owned."

Llyr's expression became hard. "He kissed you?"

"Why are you getting upset? It's not like I'd even met you." She crossed her hands over her chest. "It's not like I run around the countryside looking for men to kiss."

"This Var dared to touch you without your permission?" Llyr breathed hard. With each passing second she could see his anger rising. "I'll kill him. I'm going to hunt his stinking cat-shifting ass down and I'm going to string him up and kill him!"

When Mede realized his anger was not directed at her, she relaxed. "It was nothing. Less than nothing. It's certainly nothing to go to war over."

"He took advantage of you." Llyr balled his hands into fists.

"And I can take care of myself." Mede placed her hand on his chest and gave him a stern look. She felt his heart thudding wildly beneath her fingers. His fierceness excited her even as his protectiveness irritated her.

"I know you can take care of yourself, it's just you're—"

"A woman?" She pushed his chest. He swayed slightly but didn't stumble.

"My woman." The words were soft and he looked down at his hands. He nervously reached as if to stick them in his pocket.

Mede grabbed his hands and held them between hers. The arrogant possessiveness men normally carried when they said such things was not in his voice. She knew he was capable of both arrogance and possessiveness, but he didn't look at her like an object to be had. His eyes held a stirring passion for her.

Mede took a deep breath. She could have reminded him that she belonged to no man. She could have said his crystal was dormant. She could have laughed and put on a brave face. Instead, she did none of those things. At their stillness, some of the bioluminescent stardust came closer and fluttered around them.

"Mede, I have to tell you—"

"Shh." She shook her head. "No more talking. Look where we are."

He didn't look at the cave. Instead his gaze roamed her face. Mede dropped his hands and leaned to kiss him. A low moan escaped her as he slid his tongue over her lips, parting them. She inhaled deeply and his scent filled her. She wasn't one to run from adventure and she always went after what she wanted. In this moment, this was what she wanted, he was who she wanted.

The passion surged between them in a frenzy of pulled clothing and eager caresses. Llyr lifted her shirt over her head. He paused to take in the undergarment she wore. A band of material wrapped her to support the weight of her breasts, covering her from upper chest to waist. A low groan of approval escaped him as he cupped his palm over the sensitive mound of flesh. He skimmed the nipple still hidden beneath the binding cloth before hooking his fingers along the top edge to tug the support strap from her shoulder. As if unwrapping a gift, he drew the material slowly down her body as he knelt before her. When he pulled her undergarment, he also took hold of her pants and drew them along her legs, so that she stood mostly naked. Mede used her toes to slip out of her boots and kick her clothing aside.

Llyr surged back to his feet. That first contact of hot male flesh to her naked body was a shock of pleasure and sensitive surprise. He held her tight. The heavy lift and fall of his breathing moved his chest against hers. She felt the hard press of his member against her stomach. Mede was raised on a planet of male shifters. She wasn't completely innocent as to the male form and function. Instinct filled in what she lacked in actual knowledge.

Her body took over completely. Hands roamed him—solid arms and neck, hot chest, the indent of his spine. Lips sucked at his tongue and mouth. Hips searched forward to rub the hard length beneath his pants.

Mede found his scar before moving lower to grab his ass by sliding her fingers down the back of his breeches. He groaned and reached for his waist to unfasten the drawstring. The material slithered down his hips. Unable to help her curiosity, she broke the kiss and looked down. Llyr used the moment to push off his boots with his toes and kick the material from around his feet.

The thick shaft stood tall and leaned forward as if pointing at her stomach. She reached for him, touching the firm, smooth erection. His breath caught. Mede used her free hand to cup his neck and bring him forward. They kissed again, but this time the movements were hampered by hard breaths. She wasn't sure who started the descent to the ground, but they both moved in unison to kneel on a bed roll.

Mede pushed him so that he lay on his back. She slithered her body against his, enjoying the full contact. Llyr drew his knee between her legs to rock against her sex. The moist heat of her body helped her slide, and she jolted at the intense pleasure the gesture caused. She made a weak noise and stiffened.

Llyr rolled her onto her back. Within moments, he was between her legs, pushing his hips forward to sink his shaft into her. The hard press contrasted her feminine softness, forcing her sex to yield. He lifted on his arms to brace his weight as he penetrated her even deeper. Mede clawed at his chest as she took in the fullness of him. The stretching hurt, but she found the pleasure outweighed all else. Adventure excited her and what was this if not an adventure? Her heart raced, her breath became ragged, her body quivered, her nerves tingled, her sex ached.

"I did not imagine this would feel so…" Llyr closed his eyes tightly and moaned. He slid fully inside her and pressed his hips flush to her parted thighs. She could actually feel her pulse pounding in her sex. When he didn't move, she wiggled beneath him. Llyr opened his eyes. His lips curled as if the action had caused him physical pain.

He began to move inside her, shallow at first as if both testing a rhythm and savoring the moment. The thrusts fulfilled the innate need inside her sex and she drew her hips back and up to encourage his movements. Soon he was quickening his pace and digging his hips forward so hard that their skin slapped loudly.

"By all the gods, don't stop," Mede cried. The tiny lights danced around his head, framing his sexy body. Her breasts bounced, holding his fiery gaze. The shift of gold radiated from his eyes and she imagined hers looked much the same as his— liquid and hot and full of passion. "So help me I'll kill you if you stop."

Llyr pumped his hips harder. He growled violently, opening his mouth to bite at the air, as if the fact that he couldn't touch her breasts and maintain their bodies' rhythm frustrated him greatly. Mede had never felt anything so intense, not even when she'd explored her body and learned its workings. Had she known an orgasm could be so powerful she would have probably found a bed partner long before now. However, she didn't think the other dragons would make her feel as good as Llyr did.

She stiffened, arching her back as she came. The tremors took over, shaking her to the core. She gasped, a sharp, high-pitched sound of release. Llyr thrust a few more times before seating himself hard and firm inside her. His body jerked forcefully. For the longest time they were unable to move. When finally their breathing calmed and he pulled out of her, he fell onto his back. The frenzy of their love-making had excited the glowing creatures and they swarmed overhead, visually playing out the contra-diction of chaos and serenity she felt inside. Her bones undoubtedly turned to liquid. Her muscles relaxed. Llyr must have experienced the same sensations because he barely moved, only to place his hand over hers.

Neither of them spoke. What was there to say after such an event? Mede stared up at the dancing stars and smiled. For the first time in her life, she did not regret being born a woman.

VAR PALACE's Dining Hall

"We have something. I felt it." Attor glared at his father as the man dared to laugh at him. He'd been a fool to think he could tell the king of his plans to marry the dragon-shifter.

"You want to mate with a dragon?" King Auguste grabbed his giant belly as it jiggled in merriment. "You want to put one of those dragons on my throne?"

"It won't be yours for long," Attor mumbled. He traced his finger over the tiny scar that was developing along his forearm where Mede had cut him.

The comment wasn't quiet enough because the king heard him. Instantly, his father shifted and lunged at him. There was surprising strength left in the man's thick frame. His light brown fur spread out over his features, hiding the redness of his nose and the dark circles under his eyes. He threw Attor into the wall. "You think you can threaten me, boy? You think you're man enough to take my throne?"

Attor flinched, hating himself for shaking with fear before his father's shifted face. He stayed pressed into the wall. When shifted into a cat, his father almost looked like his old self—fierce and proud. The mask of fur hid the signs of gluttony beneath, but could not trim the stomach rounded from drink.

"That's what I thought," King Auguste dismissed with a mocking wave of his hand. He let the shift fade from his body. "Why would the most powerful woman born to this planet even want you? I'm sure the Draig have plans for her. Why would I want to connect our houses? They leave us alone. We leave them alone. The planet has been at peace. Why change what is working?"

Attor didn't bother mentioning that this system wasn't working for many of the old house nobles like Lord Myrddin. He forced himself to stand straight, though he didn't step forward. "She does want me. She even kissed me when I met her in the forest. She wanted to stay with me, but I made her go back so we could do this properly. I can't go and seek her out through royal channels without your blessing. So, I'm asking for it."

The prince's guards had failed to locate her. If his father said no, Attor would keep looking for her on his own. However, the Draig royals would be able to find her much faster and would save him the headache of a search.

"You want my blessing to go to the dragon king and ask him to send the Draig-born woman to be your bride? That is not how they do things. They wait for their crystal glow to show them their path." The king grunted and moved to the table to grab a drink. "King Tared won't command someone to marry you just because you're a Var prince who wishes it to be so."

"I did make her crystal glow," Attor lied. He didn't remember seeing a stone, but then he hadn't really looked for it. The Draig were primitive, superstitious people. He would hardly bow to the will of their make-believe gods.

That caused his father's expression to change. "It did? You're certain?"

"Yes." Attor braved a step closer. "Their gods have already blessed the match. Now I just need your blessing, my king." He knew his father's ego would like being on the same level as gods, even pretend dragon gods.

It worked, because his father slowly nodded. "Why not? If it is to be so, let it be so. You have my permission to retrieve the Draig woman and make her your mate."

"I'll leave for the Draig palace at once to make my request." Attor tried to leave but his father stopped him.

"No. If it is as you say, you will go to their Breeding Festival when night comes to the land, and you will claim her there. If you want to marry a dragon you'd better make sure that you follow their custom, so they can't dispute the match later and use it as an excuse to declare war. After the ceremony, you bring her back here and then it will be your responsibility to make sure she knows how to act like a Var lady, not a heathen dragon."

It was a small concession, but Attor hated making it nonetheless. The one night a year? That wouldn't happen for weeks yet. He didn't want to wait for her. He wanted to claim her now. He ground out between his teeth, "As you wish, father." Unable to stand the man's presence any longer, he quickly moved toward the door.

The king snorted with laughter before calling after his son, "But let us hope the children don't look like her. I'll have the ugliest grandchildren in the entire Var kingdom!"

Attor stormed away from the mocking sound. Seeing a guard at the end of the hall, he grabbed the unsuspecting man and threw him into the wall. The surprised man stumbled, dazed from the impact of stone to his head. Attor took advantage of the moment and began punching the cat-shifter in the stomach and face as hard as he could. Only when the guard was a bloody mess on the floor, did he stop. Seeing the stunned face of a nearby maid, he flicked the blood off his fingers so that it splattered on the floor.

"Don't just gawk at me," he growled. "Get this cleaned up!"

CHAPTER 9

LLYR STRETCHED HIS LEGS, the muscles stiffening though he barely moved. A deep relaxation had settled into his bones. He let his mind drift, contemplating letting it fall back into dreams or waking up completely. Something tickled his chest and he opened his eyes.

Mede.

He lifted his head, expecting to see her hand on him. Instead, several of the stardust creatures had landed on his naked skin, covering him with their soft lights. Careful not to startle them, he slowly turned to Mede who lay next to him. They had collapsed after sex and slept deeply—so deeply they apparently hadn't moved much in the night. He expected the mines to be cooler, but the temperature felt nearly perfect.

"Mede, don't move," he whispered. "Open your eyes."

She obeyed, blinking several times as if she woke from a deep sleep, but her breathing didn't change. The fact impressed him. It was an old soldiers' pretense to wake from sleep without revealing the fact to an enemy. Though they had little use for the deception, it was a tradition soldiers passed on to young soldiers. Someone had trained Mede very well. He guessed it had been Axell.

Llyr's gaze drifted down the length of her naked body. The stardust covered her breasts and stomach and he imagined if he sat up to look they'd be on her wonderfully athletic legs. Thin transparent bodies were lined with cords of light and he saw wings flutter atop the bioluminescent frames.

Mede let go of a long breath. A smile curled her mouth as she looked at him. She slowly lifted her arms to see them. A couple of the lights flew away.

"Beautiful," she whispered, her eyes filled with wonder as she tried to bring her arm closer to better study the tiny being. "I guess this means we're in for some good luck."

Llyr couldn't resist any longer. He leaned up

and ran the back of his hand down the center of her chest. The stardust flew off their bodies toward the ceiling. Mede gave a small laugh and finally stretched her limbs.

"I think I'm already lucky," he said.

She started to speak but instead ended up turning her head in a yawn. "Mm, I think I hear someone."

"The miners coming to work," Llyr answered.

Mede sat up and looked around the floor. She reached for their clothing. "Hurry. Get dressed. The last thing I want is for someone to find out what we did."

Llyr frowned. "Would it really be so bad if people knew?"

Her unamused expression was answer enough. She tossed his shirt at him. He turned his head, not bothering to catch it as it hit his chest.

"I don't think they'll come this way," he said, though his attention was more on her legs than his words. She turned and he saw her healing scar. The lines were still tinged with red and he well remembered how sore the marking could get. One sweep of a medical unit would have healed it, but he knew she wouldn't let him help.

"I don't want to risk it." She frantically turned in circles looking for her boots. Finding one several feet away, she went after it and gathered it in her arms with the rest of her clothes. "I like not having the idea of mating and marriage over our heads, but if people find out what we're doing, then the expectations start. They'll expect us to be destined. Then they'll expect us to be married. And when they see I don't make your crystal glow—*where is my other boot?*"

He slowly pulled on his shirt and watched her hurriedly jerk on her clothing as if the enemy was at the gate waiting to invade.

"I've spent way too much time earning my place. I don't want to be a bride. I don't want other men thinking of me as a potential lover." She fumbled with the drawstring at her waist. Suddenly, she stopped, "Oh, then there is my mother. Did you know some idiot told her about the Dead Dragons and that I was a member? Idiots frustrate the netherworld out of me."

"Frustrate the what?"

"The netherworld. It's something my mother says. Victorian cursing at its—" She suddenly stopped. "I know my boot did not just walk away on its own. Anyway, anyone who's met my mother should know better than to gossip about things like that to her. I can just imagine news of us getting back to her. She'll cry for a century over my maidenhead."

"Really? Why?" Llyr frowned. "I'm sure you exaggerate."

"It's her culture. They're big into the virginal bride thing." She slipped on one boot and began walking around looking for the other. Llyr reached behind his back, pulled out the missing footwear and held it up. She didn't see it right away, so he merely waited for her to look in his direction. "Oh, there it is." Mede crossed over to him and took the boot.

"So all men and women are untouched when they marry?" Llyr asked, strangely fascinated by the custom.

Mede gave a small laugh. "Just the women, not the men. Men are not held to the same virginal standard as women. They have very set gender rules. Men rule the outside. Women rule the home. If you think the Draig are strict as to male and female roles, you haven't met the Victorian colonists."

"That hardly seems fair." Llyr didn't bother to stand as he pulled his pants over his legs. He lay on his back and pushed up his hips before lacing the ties at his waist.

"Exactly." She turned her back to him, not looking at him, but not really doing anything else as she added, "It's not like you're going to be a virgin groom at your wedding."

"Not anymore," he agreed.

"I mean, you've probably had more woman than you can…" Her words stopped suddenly and she turned to look at him. "Did you just say 'not anymore'? Was last night…? Was I…?"

Llyr chuckled at her surprise. He'd known his whole life he was meant to be with her. How could he have gone to another woman? Yes, aliens had offered, but he'd never been tempted. "Is that so hard to believe?"

"But you're the prince. I know for a fact Rolant has been with—I mean, I overheard him talking to some of the other men about the women who offer themselves to the royal males." Mede looked confused, as if she wanted to believe him but didn't see how it was possible. She picked up his shoes and carried them to him. "And you were so good at it."

"Thank you," he drawled, reaching for the footwear. "You were good at it, too. Should I suspect I wasn't your first?"

"Of course you were," she dismissed. Then, smiling, she said, "You think I was good?"

Now dressed, he stood and crossed to her. He touched her cheek. "Yes, Mede, very talented." Llyr moved to kiss her, wanting her again. His cock twitched with the reminder of their shared pleasure.

Mede pulled back. "We should pack up the gear and get out of here."

"You weren't concerned about what other people thought yesterday when you came here with me." Disappointment filled him.

"That was before we became lovers. It's different now." She rolled up the bedrolls and shoved them into his pack. "And I did tell you I didn't want my reputation ruined."

"It's not like anyone will know unless you tell them…or unless they caught us in the act."

"They'll smell it," she said, sniffing her arm. "We should bathe. Or go running to erase the scent."

She had a point. Her scent lingered on his body. It was glorious and he wasn't ready to wash it off. A part of him was hurt by her insistence they hide what they were. How could she not feel their connection? Shouldn't she have suspected his crystal was a fake?

"There's a waterfall that way. Just follow the path. We can clean up there. The miners are working in a completely different section." Llyr gestured to an opening opposite the way they had entered.

Mede carried the pack and followed his direction. With a small laugh, she called, "Your pocket is glowing. Some of the stardust are hitching a ride."

Llyr looked down. The crystal had become unwrapped. He pulled it out of his pocket and tried to lift it up to show her, but she'd gone on ahead. Sighing, he placed it back in the dark cloth and once again hid it. Mede needed to come to the realization on her own. Something deep inside him knew it for a fact. It was the only way she would trust her feelings and accept their fate. Otherwise, she might do to his crystal what she'd done to hers —destroy it to stop the mating process from completing. As much as he wanted to trust in fate and the gods, he was too scared to show her the truth.

MEDE WASN'T sure why she walked so fast through the cave. For some reason she found it hard to breathe when she stood too close to Llyr. She focused her shifted eyes forward, ignoring the fat six-legged insects that hid in the crevices, and only jumped out to snack on the smaller pale lizards that ran across her path. It didn't take much concentration to hear the water, and without any turns it was easy to find her way. Llyr's footsteps behind her caused her to walk faster.

The sound of the water became louder, a

steady thundering rush. Llyr's footsteps increased their pace. Mede's heartbeat quickened slightly. Light greeted her and she no longer needed her shifted eyes to see. Cool air kissed her skin as she entered a chamber.

The waterfall she'd detected outside the cave spilled over the chamber's opening, creating a moving wall illuminated by outside light. Most of the water flowed down the side of the mountain, but some rained into the cave to feed a pool that covered most of the floor. Moss hung in thick ropes from the walls and natural columns. They were green and thick near the water spray where the sun shone through the cascade.

Llyr captured her from behind. The bag slipped from her shoulder and fell on the hard stone floor with a thud. He wrapped around her waist and pulled her tight against him. A shiver worked over her body and she closed her eyes.

Mede didn't understand their connection. Her rational mind would try to reason it, but when he touched her, she forgot herself. Maybe it was the newness of having a lover. Maybe years of her mother's hoping had finally wormed its way into her brain without her knowing it. Maybe now that she finally became a Dead Dragon, her mind needed a new adventure and it had chosen Llyr.

They were not fate.

They were not chosen by the gods.

They were not meant to be forever.

But then…

"Don't run from me," Llyr whispered.

Mede's heart raced at his words. There was a softness to them, almost a plea that stirred deep emotion. Trying to sound confident and pretty sure she was failing, she managed, "Why? Don't think you're up to the chase?"

He slid his hand upward to her neck, so that his arm rested between her breasts. The arm around her waist became a steel vice as he held her tight to his body. The evidence of his desire pressed into her backside.

"I feel your heart racing." He splayed his fingers over her neck. His voice lowered to a seductive timbre. "I feel your lungs heaving for breath. I don't think you want to run, my lady."

"Mede," she corrected automatically, as breathless as he'd indicated.

"I think you want to feel me again." Llyr rocked his hips. "You want me inside you. You want my scent on you. You want that pleasure. Say it. Tell me to release you, my lady."

"But if you release me, prince, then you won't be able to do all those things. I might escape," she teased.

A low growl revealed the sound of the dragon in his tone. The hand from her waist instantly slid down so his fingers pressed between her thighs, up to her sex. He massaged her through her pants. She trembled as pleasure worked its way through her.

Forget her rational mind. What did it know anyway?

"You want the release of my cock." Llyr burrowed his face into her hair and his breath fanned the nape of her neck. She shivered and tiny bumps rose up on her skin.

She nodded, barely able to eke out, "Yes."

Llyr pulled her shoulder, forcing her to spin around in his arms. His chest stopped her momentum as she crushed up against him. Warm lips pressed to hers. Their hands became a frenzy of movement as they undressed. Clothing flew around the cave. She vaguely heard a splash behind her but chose to ignore it. Whatever it was could wait.

She wanted more of him. The feel of his hands and mouth weren't enough. He wrapped his arms around her as if he would devour her whole.

LLYR COULDN'T CONTROL HIMSELF. He'd meant only to go after her so that they may bathe and leave the cave, but his body acted outside the will of his mind. One look at her by the water and he'd been forced to capture her.

Soft flesh mingled with defiant will to create one frustratingly perfect woman. How could he resist? Llyr might be the future king, but he'd bow to this woman every time. If she would but have him, she would control the Draig half of the planet, because she would control him.

Llyr knew this as certainly as he knew anything. Of course these were words that would never be spoken. A king couldn't admit such things. But he felt the truth of them.

Grabbing her by her naked ass, he lifted her off the ground. She wrapped her legs around his waist. Llyr tried to keep kissing her as he looked for a good spot. The ground was a course combination of damp sand and patches of mud. It clung to his feet and made for an unworthy bed. Without testing the water, which he imagined would be fairly cold, he didn't want to take her swimming and risk killing the erection now pressed between them. Opting for a cavern wall, he carried her to it and pressed her back to the moss-cushioned stone.

Llyr kept hold of her legs. Mede grasped at the vines hanging behind her head before wrapping the thick cord around her wrist to help support her weight. Within seconds he had himself aimed to take her. Seeing a breast close to his lips, he moaned. He opened his mouth wide and took a gentle bite. The nipple puckered against his tongue as he sucked it. The moist heat of her sex called to him and he thrust hard. A high-pitched noise escaped her at the claim.

He moved inside her, unable to help the frantic drive of his hips. Desperately, he needed her to feel what he did, to know what he knew and to admit to her feelings. That desperation manifested as wild passion.

The slick hold of her body sheathed him perfectly. Everything about her was made for him. Her breast slipped from his mouth.

Llyr gripped her thighs and leaned his forehead to touch hers. Mede panted. Her gaze held his, her eyes swirling with a shift.

The pleasure came over them hard, climaxing in a dizzying explosion that nearly dropped him to his knees. He pressed her back into the stone as his muscles stiffened. Mede pulled on the vine. He saw her arm flex seconds before the plant snapped. The sudden release of her weight caused him to stumble backwards. His foot slid in the mud and she rode his body to the ground.

The hard grit of sand scraped his naked ass. Mede straddled his waist, bouncing on his cock when they landed. She made a strange groaning noise as her body jerked violently. Her hands pressed to his chest as she shook again, still finding release.

A stunned, short laugh escaped her. "Are you injured?"

"I don't know." Llyr shifted his hips. The movement on his cock still inside her caused a tiny spasm of release. He closed his eyes and moaned at the pleasure.

"I think maybe we should rethink our positioning next time."

Llyr opened an eye. "Next time?"

"I need a new adventure," she whispered, leaning over to kiss the tip of his nose. "Until we're forced to go to the Breeding Ceremony to look for mates, you're it."

"So you are going to the ceremony?" He let his hands move up her hips.

"I have to attend. I don't have to marry." Mede moved to stand. She winced as her legs straightened. Her knees were scraped from the fall. She silently offered to help him up.

Llyr reached to brush the sand from his ass. The flesh stung. "There's a medic unit in the bag."

"Clean up first," Mede said. She walked to the water and skimmed a toe over the top. "You don't want the medic healing bits of sand into your flesh.

I like your ass as it is. No need to morph that pretty finish into something resembling a shaved yorkin."

"As my lady wishes," Llyr answered.

Mede arched a brow, but this time she didn't correct his use of the title.

CHAPTER 10

"THE KING SENT a runner to summons you back to the palace immediately," Tomos said. He kept his eyes averted from Mede as he looked at Prince Llyr. "He did not say why, only that there is a royal matter requiring your attendance."

"Was there no hint?" Llyr asked.

"None," Tomos said. "Only that you are to make the trip immediately."

Mede watched the two men with interest. Llyr had managed to lead her out of the cave without incident. The miners could be heard working in a different chamber, away from where they walked. When they'd emerged, Tomos had been lounging against a boulder waiting for them.

Llyr nodded and then turned to her. "Join me?"

"At the palace?" Mede shook her head in instant denial. "No."

"Tomos is staying here with his family," Llyr insisted. "I'd like the company."

Mede glanced at Tomos who seemed surprised by the plan. Her voice a little too high, she answered, "No. I think I'll go home to help my mother…do…some things. It's not a long run to the palace. The paths are easy. You'll be fine."

"As prince, you shouldn't travel alone," Tomos said. "Burden of the crown."

Llyr nodded at him. Mede gave Tomos a hard look. The man lifted his hands and backed away from her. He walked several paces ahead on the path, leaving them to some privacy.

"Are you scared of the palace?" Llyr arched a brow.

"I'm not scared of anything." Mede stiffened.

"I'm not so sure. You've been avoiding royal invitations for some time now."

Mede bit her lip. Lowering her voice, she asked, "So they've noticed?"

"My parents? Yes, of course the king and queen have noticed the only female dragon on the planet has slighted the queen's invitation by sending excuses in her stead. Repeatedly."

Mede stepped closer. One of her boots had been tossed into the pool when they undressed and now it squished every time she put weight on her right foot. She turned her head away from Tomos' direction, to whisper, "Was the queen upset?" She thought of her mother, crying in disappointment at something Mede had failed to do.

Llyr didn't answer and she couldn't read his expression.

"If you insist I make an appearance at the palace, I will go." She straightened her shoulders and tried to act unconcerned. They had bathed, but her clothes weren't really fit for the royal court. Maybe if she made a bad impression, the queen would not invite her back. That thought didn't make her as happy as it should have. She wanted them to like her. Not simply because they were the king and queen, but she wanted Llyr's parents to like her.

"Wonderful." Llyr grabbed her elbow gently urging her to fall into step beside him. "The queen will be very pleased." He dropped her arm and patted Tomos on the shoulder as they moved past him. "See you at the festival, Tomos. Good luck finding a bride."

Mede gave Tomos a strained smile. The water-logged boot made an audible *squish-squish-squish* noise as she walked after Llyr. The palace? What had she gotten herself into?

THE RUN to the palace was easier in shifted form. Llyr wouldn't admit it, but the summons worried him. His parents hadn't called him back to the palace since he was a child. He checked in regularly, knew his diplomatic schedule, and sneaked away during his free time to hunt or camp, or more recently to pursue his future bride. Needlessly glancing over his shoulder, he confirmed what he already knew. Mede was there, shifted and running barefoot over the rough terrain. He'd offered to find her shoes but she'd just laughed at him, saying her boot would dry faster if she carried it.

There were no clouds in the green-tinted heavens and the suns shone bright and hot, but Mede did not complain—not that he expected she would. The wide red and gray path they traveled was a direct route to the palace near the base of the mountains. Spear-shaped peaks shot up from the land behind them like a warning from the earth, becoming gentler as they headed south into the foothills. The farther they traveled, the redder the ground became, until the gray disappeared altogether.

The feelings of dread did not dissipate as he neared the palace, though he could not fathom why he should be apprehensive. He wanted Mede to meet his parents. By all rights, he should be excited by the fact. Instead, he had the most overwhelming urge to order her home.

"Someone's coming," Mede said, slowing her run to a walk. When he glanced back at her, she'd shifted to human form but her eyes glowed as she listened to the distance. "One man."

Llyr heard it as well. "We're near the palace. It's probably a guard."

"No. It's Rolant," Mede said. "I spent hours running with him during my initiations. I know his stride."

As if to prove her point, Llyr's brother appeared on the path. Mede had a good ear. Llyr nodded, impressed.

Rolant gave him a tight smile and nodded in greeting before turning to Mede. Instantly, he froze. Charging to Llyr, he demanded, "Gods' bones, Llyr, why did you bring her?"

Mede gasped in obvious shock.

"I'm taking her to the palace." Llyr glared at his brother in warning. Rolant glanced at Llyr's neck where he still wore the wrong stone. "The queen has wanted to meet her for some time."

"Don't you know what's happened?" Rolant asked, his body remaining tense. "I thought you came back for—"

"Father sent a runner to find me. He just said

there was an important matter that I needed to attend to," Llyr answered.

"What's going on, Rolant?" Mede inquired, coming to stand beside the brothers.

"Cynan is gone," Rolant said. "Two days now. Saben and Dylan found his abandoned campsite and Saben tracked a party of Var shifters into the shadowed marshes near Lord Myrddin's fortress."

"What you're suggesting is an act of war," Mede said. "Do you think Lord Myrddin had anything to do with this? I know he hates us, but would he dare?"

"We have no proof beyond his men patrolling closer to our borders since your run," Rolant said. "That blond fur had to come from someone at the palace. I don't know why, but most of the blond-furred cats are recruited as palace guards. I suppose it's to match the décor?"

"Did the cat-shifter give you any clue as to his identity?" Llyr thought of what she'd told him, of how the man had taken liberties and kissed her. The primal dragon in him wanted to find the palace guard and beat him for it. The more logical, albeit barely, male in him held the dragon back from such possessively dominant shows of love.

Mede shook her head. "He was just a Var running in the forest near the marsh farmer. He was well groomed and spoke eloquently, but after

Owain anything would have looked well groomed. He might have been protecting someone else in the forest. I heard a woman and man…"

"What?" Rolant demanded.

"They were coupling," she mumbled weakly. "Maybe the guard was there as protection? He said the woman was an offworlder and they weren't married. Maybe the prince was running around the forest with someone who was not his wife? I heard married Var men often sleep with women they're not married to."

"It's called half mating." Rolant frowned. "But the royals don't half mate, not that I've ever heard of. Is Prince Attor even married?"

"I don't believe he is." Llyr turned to Mede. "I don't see the prince leaving the luxury of the palace to have a liaison. I have heard he is a bit…"

"Delicate," Rolant supplied.

"Yeah, delicate," Llyr repeated, though that was putting it nicely. By all accounts, and by the few meetings he'd had with the man, the Var prince was a spoiled child. King Auguste had even indicated in conversation that Attor was a weakling. "Gods help the cats the day that man comes into power. You might have heard an old house noble. They are the true threat. The king is more of a figurehead."

"That's all that happened." Mede gave Llyr a

pleading look. He wasn't about to tell anyone about the kiss. "We heard the couple. I got the fur. I left. Now what is this about Cynan?" Mede brought the subject back around to the missing dragon. The worry was evident on her face. "And why don't you want me here?"

"The king has assembled the Dead Dragons. Since Cynan is one of our own we are to go after him. Any of us within a five minute run of the palace is to be gathered for the search party."

"Yes, of course," Mede answered. "Let's go now."

"Mede, this isn't a run to skin a cat," Llyr said. "This isn't going to be friendly. We don't know what's happening."

"More reason for us to get going," Mede ground out tightly. "I've trained my whole life for battle. I'm not scared. I don't want war, but if I'm called to battle I'll go. I will not dishonor my family name."

"I forbid it." Llyr knew the mistake of his words the instant he said them, but he didn't want to take them back. "It is too dangerous."

"You have no right to forbid me from going. You're not my parent and I'm not a child. You're not my king. You're not my anything. You're the prince who should be more worried about answering your father's summons to the palace than lecturing me on what I can and cannot do. I *am* a Dead Dragon. I have rightfully earned my place. And Cynan is not only a brother dragon, he is my friend." She turned to Rolant. "And you, how dare you try to leave me behind in the mountains. I'll find the others and ready myself."

Mede stormed away from them. Llyr moved to follow her but Rolant grabbed his arm and jerked him back. "She's right, you know. You have no authority to stop her now that she is here."

Llyr reached into his pocket to hold up the stone. "This gives me the authority. She's my—"

"Your what?" Rolant demanded. "You haven't even told her. And you are not her husband. She has to choose you first."

"Send her home," Llyr commanded.

"I told you not to let her get marked. I warned you to stop it when you had a chance. Now it's out of my hands. She's one of us and I can't play favorites. Ancient tradition and the king's decree dictate otherwise." Rolant placed a hand on his shoulder. "She is here. She is coming. I'll protect her as I would any of my brothers."

"I'm coming with you." Llyr made a move to follow Mede.

"No." Rolant grabbed his arm hard and squeezed. "You go to the palace. I have the impression there is more happening here than just

Cynan. Find out what. Protect our people. Do your duty."

"If she goes, I go." Llyr jerked his arm from Rolant's grasp.

"You know it is not the same for you. You're our future king and commander and are needed at the palace. This is one mission you can't join us on."

"I'm not scared of the Var," Llyr denied, even though he knew is brother was right. He'd earned his mark into their order, but he was held to a higher duty first—ruling a planet. Unless they were to go to actual war, he was not to participate in fights. No one would think less of him for not going. In fact, if he did go they might think he didn't care about his people's future. But what of his future, his Mede?

"You know better than to think like that." Rolant frowned. "Our father would not have sent the order unless the situation was serious. There has to be more to this than Cynan going missing."

Llyr hated his current circumstances.

"Go to the palace and find out." Rolant shoved his shoulder to get him moving.

Llyr slowly nodded. "Find Cynan and bring him home. And, Mede, please…"

Rolant nodded. "If necessary I'll give my life for hers, Llyr, I swear it."

Llyr already knew as much. Rolant ran after Mede to where the Dead Dragons would have gathered. He stared at the place where his brother had disappeared into the tree line. Everything inside told him to go after them. But if he did, he'd dishonor himself by defying their laws. And, worse, he'd dishonor Mede by implying she didn't deserve to stand alongside men.

"By all the gods, keep her safe," Llyr whispered after his brother. Is this how wives felt when the Draig soldiers went off to battle? The gripping fear and panic he couldn't show the world? The desires of the man warred with the duty of a prince. "I beg you, whatever it takes keep her safe."

Crossing the border into Var land for the second time was nothing like Mede's first run. Before, it was only her pride that mattered. Now, Cynan's life was on the line. The man might already be dead. No one knew why the Var had taken him. Cynan often camped in the woods outside the palace, living off the land and always opening his tent to a friend.

She couldn't think about Llyr, or how frustratingly mad he'd made her when he'd doubted her abilities in front of Rolant. He'd actually tried to order her home because it was too dangerous.

"Save your anger for the Var," Rolant whispered, coming to a stop near her. He didn't shift back to human, instead speaking to her in the Qurilixian language. They ducked behind a tree, waiting for the signal to continue forward. "I know my brother can be a pain but he means well."

"I don't know what you are talking about," Mede lied, also not bothering to shift back. She needed her senses on full alert.

"Then you weren't just cursing him under your breath just now?" Rolant gave a small laugh. He was trying to lighten her mood, but she saw the worry around his eyes.

"Perhaps I was." Mede held up her hand to end the conversation and then nodded to the far brush where she saw a flicker of movement within the leafy cluster.

Rolant followed her gaze. For a long moment, they held still. Someone ahead of them made a small whistle and a bird flew from the brush. She relaxed her guard and stood to continue forward.

The green of her clothes blended with the surroundings, as did the brown of her armored skin. Var were at a disadvantage when shifted in the marshes, for their colorful fur didn't always lend itself to hiding. So far they had traveled with little incident, following Saben's lead to where the trail ended.

They were close to the marshes, so close there were times they were forced to step into the putrid water. Nests of snakes squirmed in muddy burrows, warning them of how dangerous the water really was. Mede leapt over a particularly thick grouping, vaulting over the red and black tailed givre only to slide upon landing across a muddy plateau. Luckily, she retained her footing and didn't make the journey on her backside.

"Careful marking the ground." Rolant commanded. Mede grimaced. She already knew, but couldn't say anything to dispute his reprimand. The slip had been an accident. He nodded over the swamp to where she could just make out a stone wall rising up over water. "Myrddin's fortress." Moss a sickly shade of yellow-green that reminded her of pus and infection clung to the castle. From what she'd heard of Myrddin, it was a fitting scene for the man was a walking infection.

Rolant led her away from the fortress. Seeing the other dragons gathered next to a small outcropping near drier land, they moved to join them.

"I smell wet cat." Arthur touched the tip of his crooked nose.

"Myrddin's castle fortress is right over there," Rolant said.

"Whoever took Cynan camped back there," Saben pointed north from whence they'd come and then moved his fingers to point southeast, "but they continued on that way."

"That's away from the fortress." Rolant frowned. "So we are not blaming the old house nobles?"

"What about the marsh farmer?" Mede asked. "The still I found wasn't too far from here. He was angry that we kept knocking over his batch of liquor. I don't see him being able to formulate the plan, but if he has friends…"

"I thought the same thing," Saben answered. "I checked the stills after the trail went cold. There was no evidence those drunks did anything more than pass out somewhere in the forest."

"Myrddin could have left the trail to throw us off and then doubled back here to the fortress," Arthur said.

"I don't trust Myrddin, but we follow the trail," Rolant said, his decision made. "If we storm the gates now and Cynan is not there, we lose any chance we have of finding him."

"Agreed." Saben nodded once and stood to lead the group away from the fortress.

Not much was said as they traveled on, deeper into Var land. Mede kept sharp eyes on the ground and trees, looking for clues that a group had passed.

It was Dylan who finally picked up several tracks. The footprints were easy to follow but there was no guarantee it was the right group of Var.

"Drag marks," Saben pointed out.

"Could be a hunting party," Arthur said.

"No prey in this marsh is that large. This has to be it." Rolant didn't wait for an agreement as he quickened their pace through the trees. Mede followed without question. The apprehension she felt was shared by all, she saw it in their unusually serious expressions. But not a single person showed their fear, not a single warrior hesitated.

"They stop here." Rolant frowned, looking at the ground. They stood in a small clearing of dry land next to a rocky ledge. The forest was quiet, perhaps too quiet, but she couldn't detect the presence of the Var. "They just vanish."

Mede looked up the cliff and slowly stepped back. Directly above where the tracks ended was a small inlet in the stone. She lowered her voice to a whisper. "A cave. There."

In unison the dragon men looked upward and backed away from the cliff to see where she indicated.

"We can climb it," Saben said.

"Mede and Dylan, you are the smallest. We'll need you in case there is a tight space. You two will climb with me. The rest of you stay down here on watch," Rolant ordered before leaping to scramble up the steep rock wall. His footing slipped but he quickly righted himself. Mede and Dylan obeyed, following him up. The stone was mostly smooth and the occasional jagged pieces did not allow much in the way of handholds. As she neared the top, Rolant reached down for her arm and jerked her up and over the edge, before doing the same for Dylan.

They stood on a narrow ridge in the cave's opening. A rope ladder was coiled on the ground near the entrance. Mede kicked it down in case the others needed to fight their way up. Rolant had to shift into human form to squeeze through the narrow opening into the dim cave. His dragon body wouldn't have been pliable enough to pass.

Mede followed him, forced to use her human hands to claw her way through. "There is no way they could have brought Cynan through here."

Rolant pointed to a thick smear of blood on an interior rock.

Dylan emerged through the opening and instantly went to touch the blood. He sniffed it. "It's Draig."

LLYR LOOKED out over the forest from the office balcony. The stone railing kept him from leaping over the side. The desire to go after Mede became so strong he could barely contain it, but the fall would probably kill him. She was out there in the distant Var forest, trudging through marshes and the gods only knew what else. His talons clawed into the stone.

The palace was more fortress than grand castle. If someone looked up at him from the ground, they wouldn't see the windows or balconies attached to the royal quarters. The exterior was carefully carved to look natural, like the cliff edge of a mountain. The surrounding valley would be where the wedding festival would be held. Beyond that, the small village was nestled near the enormous trees. He could make out the rock-lined roads placed on an even grid between wooden homes. The village was a reminder as to why he couldn't go after Mede. Like all Draig villages, it was under the protection of the House of Draig, his father's house. Under his family's rule, the people of his land prospered. No one went hungry. No one went without shelter unless they wanted to. Everyone worked and contributed to the best of their abilities.

His gaze went from the village toward the Var marshlands. Prince and man. How could he choose which path to take when they led him in opposite directions? The people of his village? Or Mede, his heart, his very reason for living? Even now she might be in danger.

He clawed the stone harder, scratching it in his frustration. At the sound of one of his parents finally joining him, he turned eagerly. "I know of Cynan. I saw Rolant on my way here. What else has happened?"

Queen Lorna lifted her hands and moved forward as if to calm the wild beast brimming inside her son. She was not a dragon-shifter, but she handled the Draig well. The queen had come to Qurilixen when she was just old enough to marry. She had the dark hair and eyes of her people and did not cower from obstacles put in her path. As the only daughter of a poor Serean craftswoman, her mother had taught her to make furniture at a young age to help around the work-shop. She'd done this instead of going to school and had not known how to read anything but Serean blueprints for the first twenty years of her life. That childhood had left her with tiny scars on her hands that she never tried to hide.

"Relax, my son," the queen said. She placed her hand on his chest. "Your heart is beating too fast with worry."

"Lorna, are you in..." The king's voice always

had a raspy quality to it, as if his vocal cords had permanently locked in a half shift and affected his tone. "There you are."

King Tared was very much like Llyr—born heir to the title, passionate about his people, and protective of his family—insomuch that the two men even looked like replicas of each other, plus or minus a few battle scars. Rolant looked more like a combination of his parents, with the king's coloring and his mother's Serean features.

"What is happening? I should be with the others looking for Cynan." Llyr gestured behind him toward the borderlands.

"Good, then you know the most urgent half," the king said.

"There's more?" Llyr stepped away from the ledge.

"All know Cynan camps alone," his father put forth. "I don't think we were meant to discover he'd gone missing so quickly. It's possible he was taken for information about the Dead Dragons, or our military, or the palace. He has privileges with all three."

"Cynan would not have gone down gently." Llyr knew that much for a fact. The warrior was very strong.

"We are not sure what happened. There were drag marks at his camp. It is possible he did not even get a chance to fight." The king studied his son. "What do you know of our female dragon? This Lady Medellyn?"

"I've met her," Llyr said carefully. He guiltily thought of the stone hidden in his pocket. "She is with the Dead Dragons going after Cynan."

"You let a woman go?" King Tared's voice rose in surprise at the very notion.

"She's tougher than many men of our kind. Rolant assures me she is trained for war and she is a member of the Dead Dragons. You decreed all Dead Dragons within a five minute hard run were to be gathered for the search party." Llyr had to look away from his father's probing gaze. "You ordered her to go, my king."

"Why not a woman?" Queen Lorna demanded of her husband.

"Women are to be protected at all costs. Men are warriors. Women belong in the home under our protection. That is the way the gods created the genders." The king defended his position, but Llyr had a feeling his father would be apologizing profusely to his wife once they were alone.

Queen Lorna made an unamused humming noise but said nothing more. Yeah, his father was going to be doing a lot of begging later.

"Why do you ask about Lady Mede?" Llyr drew his parent's attention back to himself.

"I received a missive from the Var king inquiring about our female. He has requested to be allowed at our wedding festival." King Tared shook his head in disbelief. "In all my years, I have never heard of a Var being invited to attend our sacred festival. I cannot find reason for the request. We've had a female dragon for years. Why ask about her now? The timing is too close to Cynan's disappearance. Until now, I had thought King Auguste wanted our peace to last. The Var stay on their side. We stay on ours. Neither side has anything to do with the other. I like it that way. This request makes me uneasy."

Llyr's heart pounded violently. What did King Auguste want with Mede? And she was out there, at this very moment, in Var territory. Was the kidnapping a trap? "When Mede did her initiation run into the Var forest, she came back with blond fur, not the fur from a marsh farmer like most of the runners. What if that is how King Auguste heard of her? If she'd met up with someone from the royal palace, they would have told the king about it. She is beautiful and strong and makes an impression."

"There is nothing more we can do about this but wait for word about Cynan." The queen touched her husband's arm. "We should go to the temple and ask the gods to protect them. It is more productive than speculating."

"Come son." The king gestured that Llyr was to follow.

"Give me a moment," Llyr said, trying to maintain control. "I'll be along shortly."

His mother gave him a soft smile. His father gruffly nodded. They both left.

Why did the Var king want to attend the Breeding Ceremony? King Auguste had been married once, but his mate had died. He wasn't sure exactly how it worked, but the Var were not like the Draig. They didn't always mate to one woman. They could, but they could also take half mates. In theory, he supposed a Var could take a full mate, and then a half mate. The very idea was strange to Llyr. How could a man love more than one woman? How could a man marry if he wasn't completely in love? If Llyr's mate was to die, he'd never recover from the loss.

Llyr turned back to the village and the borderlands, torn worse than before. Did he risk his life to save the woman he loved, who might not even be in danger? Or did he uphold the honor of his title and do what tradition, his parents, the gods and Draig law demanded of him?

What should he choose?

How could he choose?

MEDE LIFTED her tunic shirt and drew the blade from her waist. She waited while Rolant and Dylan did the same. Her eyes shifted so she could see in the dim cave light. The stone was red like it was near the Draig palace. The tunnel opened up into a large cavern of crystal formations that refracted streams of light and turned them into prismatic rainbows of color. Small inlets revealed nothing but rock and dirt. Fresh footprints scuffed the dirty floor and they followed them east toward a lower subsystem of tunnels. Though there were possible turns, they kept on the worn trail. The tracks ended near a steep decline.

When Rolant hesitated, Mede jumped down first. The stone was damp and the air musty. She carefully stepped over tiny puddles of liquid.

Suddenly, she stopped, holding up her hand for the other two to do the same. A thick iron door had been built at the end of the tunnel, in a place where there should be no reason to have a door.

She placed her hand on it. The door moved at her touch, hitting its frame before bouncing open just enough to let light spill out into the tunnel. She listened, able to detect what could have been shallow breathing.

Rolant grabbed her arm and pulled her behind him with a look of warning. He leaned to peek into the light. Slowly, he opened the door. It moved soundlessly on its hinges. The man stepped into the light. Mede followed, ignoring the fear in her gut and the pounding of her heart.

They were in high-tech laboratory. The stone of the cave floor had been lined with metal. Chairs were pushed away from tables. Papers and files were scattered over desks. Whoever had been here was gone now.

"What is this place?" Mede asked, looking at Dylan. He moved to a computer monitor and began looking at the files.

"Is that my sister dragon, or am I hallucinating?"

Mede stiffened and rushed toward the voice. Cynan was locked in a cage next to a dead Owain. The almost non-existent smell of decay indicated the death was recent. Black liquid trails ran out of Owain's nose and eyes to puddle around the floor. It was too dark to be blood and had a strange odor to it.

"Cynan!" Mede reached for the cage door and shook it. The latch was too strong to break. To the others, she yelled, "I need a key."

"No, stop," Cynan said wearily. "You must leave this place."

"We came for you." Mede studied his face. He looked sick. Dark circles marred the flesh beneath his eyes. He coughed, too weak to lift his hand. A tiny rivulet of black liquid trailed over his chin. "What happened? Who did this?"

"Var captured me. Had to be Var. They invaded my campsite, darted me with something, and the next thing I know I wake up here next to this loud, smelly bastard surrounded by four alien scientists." Cynan's eyes moved briefly to Owain. "At least he's quiet now."

"Where did they go?" Rolant asked.

"I don't know." Cynan closed his eyes. "The scientist injected us with something. When this marsh farmer started getting sick they panicked and hauled ass out of here. Couldn't even do the decent thing and put us out of our misery."

"We're taking you home," Mede said. "Dylan, open the door."

"By all the gods," Dylan whispered. His face paled as he turned away from the monitor to look at her. "I don't think we can."

Cynan coughed again. Black came out of his nose dripping to his chest.

"Help him!" she demanded.

"There's nothing he can do," Cynan insisted. "Leave me. Seal this place behind rock."

"No." Mede shook her head in denial. Tears slipped from her eyes and she didn't care who saw them. She reached her hand into the cage, trying to touch Cynan. "Give me your hand."

"Mede, don't touch the black, it's highly contagious. He's right. We can't do anything for him. We have to leave him. This substance they injected him with, kills shifters. If we take him from here, we'll kill everyone who touches the infected person. Right now it's not airborne, but if it spreads, it's only a matter of time before it mutates and adapts…"

Mede slumped to the floor. Her hand dropped to the bottom of the cage but she didn't pull it out. She pressed her face against the bars.

"Argh!" Rolant yelled in anger, slashing his hand over the table. Little containers scattered around the laboratory. Mede ignored the tirade. Rolant only acted how she felt.

"Keep looking, Dylan," she whispered. "There

has to be a way to stop this."

"Find something," Rolant repeated the order.

A black tear trailed out of Cynan's eye. Mede wasn't sure how long she stared at him, desperately wanting to comfort him and unable to reach him. She spoke in low tones, not sure what she really said to him, only that her voice seemed to bring him some comfort. She saw his pain and wanted to take it away. The shallow rise and fall of his chest was so gentle she wasn't sure it even moved.

"We're going to avenge you," she promised the man. "They won't get away with this."

"He's gone, Mede," Rolant said, touching her shoulder.

"I'm sorry," Dylan stammered. "I tried. I…"

"It was good we could at least be here with him," Rolant stated. "No one should die alone."

Mede turned hard eyes to the prince. He is Draig. He was not meant to die in a cage. She shrugged off Rolant's hand. Turning, she eyed the laboratory. Then, seeing a white jacket, she grabbed it and pulled it to her face. The scent of a doctor was there.

She turned to Dylan. "Say the blessing. Send him to sit beside the gods. Don't leave his spirit in this place. Then lock this chamber and bury it under so much rock no one will find it for hundreds of years. Leave everything inside."

Dylan shifted and began chanting the ancient words of burial.

Mede couldn't control the dragon as it came over her in a hard ripple. She shredded the jacket in anger and tossed the pieces aside. "I'm going to hunt these aliens down and rip them apart."

She tore from the laboratory, ran through the tunnel, and then jumped up through the hole. Rolant kept pace with her. She heard his angry breathing and knew he would not try to stop her. Sprinting, she didn't stop until she was at the cave's entrance in the side of the cliff.

Mede scanned the forest from her high perch. Her eyes narrowed as she focused her vision. Birds flew in the distance as if startled. With a growl, she fell more than climbed down the rock face. The others gathered around her.

"What happened?" Arthur demanded.

"Dead," Mede managed, the word barely making it out of her throat.

"Mede?" Llyr stepped before her. The shock of seeing him froze her in place. He must have joined the group while she was in the cave. His eyes met hers in question. "What happened?"

Rolant leapt down. "Cynan's dead."

Mede breathed hard. Llyr reached for her, but she turned from him. Now was not the time for tenderness. "Dragons to arms!" she yelled, running into the forest. Without question, they followed her lead, shifting for whatever battle was to come.

Every one of her senses had focused on her task —find the alien scientists and kill them. Rage swelled inside her, driving away all thoughts of prudence. It was easier to be angry than to admit her grief. She slashed her hand at a limb, severing it with her talons. Her body moved as if of its own accord as her brain chanted for revenge.

She heard a small laugh the same moment she picked up the scent from the laboratory. The noise infuriated her. How dare they laugh? How dare they breathe?

"Laugh at me all you want. We don't deserve to live, not after what we've done," a man said. He spoke the Old Star language with a thick accent she didn't recognize. "On my home world we'd be executed for it. Death for death."

"This isn't your home world, Cragen, and we're not bound by this planet's laws. Soon we'll be gone and it won't matter," another man answered. He sounded younger than the first, with a nervous energy she could practically smell radiating through the forest. Mede followed the sound. "The stuff dies with the test subjects. No one will even know what we did. It doesn't matter. This stupid little nowhere planet doesn't matter."

"We shouldn't have taken this job," a woman

answered. "Genetic targeting is too hard. Shifter DNA is too similar and transformative by nature. Look where they put us? There is no decent city on this primitive planet."

"You're the one who said you could alter and accelerate the Black Crawl, Shann—*shh, I heard something*," a second woman said.

"You're being paranoid," the younger man scolded.

Mede burst through the trees, talons drawn. She went directly for the scent matching the jacket she'd found. A redheaded woman screamed as Mede lunged for her. The alien's shiny silver dress sparkled like a target.

Dragons sprang out of the forest. The whiz of a laser shot past her to sizzle against a tree. All of the warriors had been trained to use lasers, but they were considered a dishonorable weapon because it took little skill to point and shoot at a target. If anything, the Qurilixian preferred blades for fighting. Or talons.

"Get him!" Llyr growled.

The rage flowed through Mede and she found it hard to concentrate beyond anything but revenge. Her blood felt like the dragon lava of her dreams, burning beneath the skin. Mede's fingers wrapped the redhead's throat and she turned her captive by her neck to better see the battlefield. Another laser blast sounded. The redhead jerked as she was struck in the back. She opened her mouth to speak, but only blood came out. Mede dropped the dead weight.

Rolant and Arthur subdued a brunette by holding her arms. The woman kicked violently but the men didn't hurt her. Though one look at Rolant's face told her he wanted to rip the female apart for what she'd done. Llyr faced the scientist they'd called Cragen, who held one laser blaster pointed at the prince and one aimed to the side. The younger humanoid man was next to him, reaching to take the second weapon.

Mede swept to the side to take the men out. Her heart pounded in worry. The laser aimed at Llyr would easily pierce the dragon's armor. One shot would kill him. She watched the tip. If it fired, she could stop it with her body. No one else would die on her watch. Not today. Not Llyr. By all the gods, please not Llyr.

The man fired. Mede jumped in front of Llyr to take the blast. Llyr growled in anger and jerked her arm to pull her back into his body. Her heart beat so hard and ached so badly she thought Cragen had blown a hole in her chest. Llyr tried to turn her but she fought him, using her body to shield him from another blast. She waited for the burning pain of death, but it never came. When she glanced down, she was whole.

The younger doctor sank to his knees with a stunned look on his face. Cragen had shot his fellow scientist in the chest the moment he tried to take the blaster. The older man swung the blaster aimed at Llyr to the side and fired again, this time hitting the brunette woman subdued by Rolant and Arthur in the neck. She slumped and made a gurgling noise. The dragons dropped their hold on her.

The man was killing his own people. Mede jerked her arm from Llyr's tight grasp. She growled at the scientist to stop. They needed to know who'd hired him before they killed him.

"I don't know if you speak my language, but Shann didn't give them the right cure," Cragen said. He clearly didn't understand her dragon's voice. "The potency was all wrong. This disease is too pure in its current state and the cure wasn't strong enough to work yet. We didn't mean to kill anyone."

Mede lunged at the same time Llyr did. Llyr pushed her to the side, out of harm's way. The scientist turned the laser on his temple and blasted himself in the head before they could stop him.

Mede looked around at the dead bodies. She shook with unspent energy. This was not how she'd imagined her first battle going. Her head felt dizzy and she pushed at her temple. "What just happened?"

"They turned on themselves." Llyr's gaze bore into hers and she had to look away. "Does someone want to explain what we're doing here?"

"They…" Mede took a deep breath and closed her eyes. The rage was not gone. Seeing the scientists dead did not take away her grief. She still wanted to tear something apart.

"They killed Cynan," Rolant finished for her. "They injected him with some kind of contagion. We can't move the body or it will spread. We have to leave him in the Var cave. Dylan is taking care of it." Rolant turned to Arthur and Saben. "I'll show you the way. We need to help Dylan bury the laboratory once he's done with the burial rites."

"Laboratory? In the cave?" Arthur questioned as Rolant quickly led them away. They left her alone with Llyr.

"Are you a fool? That shot was meant for me!" Llyr growled, spinning her around to face him. She stumbled, not ready for the sudden motion of her body.

A tear slipped from her eye to slide down her cheek. The shift faded from her body to leave her drained of energy. "Don't question me. I am in no mood to defend myself. I did what I had to do—protect the future king."

"The future king?" he questioned. Llyr too shifted to human form. "Is that all?"

"Yes." She gave a weak nod. No. No, that wasn't all. The idea of him dying was more than she could handle. The fear she'd felt in that second tried to work its way back up her throat. If she lost him…if she lost Llyr… Mede looked at the bodies before moving to follow the others. She couldn't breathe when she looked at Llyr. "Let them rot where they fell. They don't deserve a burial blessing."

"Mede, stop, tell me what happened. You don't seem like yourself."

"What are you doing here? You're supposed to be at the palace," she said at the same time.

"A dragon was in trouble. I wasn't going to sit at the palace and wait." Llyr followed her for several paces before trying to step in front of her to stop her.

"That is exactly what you should have done, prince." Mede growled at him. "You don't belong out here. You are the future of the kingdom. That is more important than any…thing." She thought of Cynan, not so sure of her statement. "There is nothing for you to do here. You should have reported to the palace like the king decreed."

"I did report to the palace. My father told me of Cynan's kidnapping, the Var's suspected involvement, and warned me of Lord Myrddin's men along our borders. There was also an unusual request from the Var king."

"What request?"

Llyr shook his head. "I'm not allowed to speak of it."

"Then why mention it?"

"Because…" He ran his hands through his hair in frustration. "Because I…"

"What are you doing here, prince? You're the future king. Go find a throne." Mede pushed him. Her throat and stomach burned as if she'd swallowed a torch, or a batch of her own cooking. She pressed a fist to her chest, trying to will the heartburn down. "You're not supposed to run into danger. What if you were infected? What if you were shot? What would I do then? I mean the people. What would the people do then?"

"Then Rolant would step up," he yelled back. His voice echoed and he took a deep breath to calm himself. More carefully, he continued, "I'm not just a future king, Mede. I'm a man. I'm a Dead Dragon. Cynan is—*was*—my brother, too. I know my duty and I went to the palace and I did it. And when it was done I came for you, Mede."

"For me?" Mede took a step back to put

distance between them. "I don't need a man's protection."

"I'm not here because you're a woman who needs my protection. I know you can handle yourself as a dragon." Llyr's tone pleaded with her, trying to make her understand something. She wasn't sure what though. Everything was too confusing. "I came because I had to. I came because I love you."

She gave a short laugh to choke back tears. The words would have brought her pleasure if they hadn't made him chase her into danger, if the evidence of their falsehood wasn't so clearly seen in his dormant crystal.

"Did you hear me, my lady? I love you. When you jumped in front of me it nearly killed me. I love you." Llyr tried to move closer but she lifted her hand to stop him. "Gods' bones, woman, I'm telling you I love you. Say something."

Mede slowly licked her lips, trying to get them to stop trembling. If only his words were true. She shook her head. "Look at your crystal. You can't love me. I'm just the only woman you've ever known. Maybe sex was a," her breath caught but she managed to finish, "a bad idea. It confused things between us."

"This isn't my crystal. You do make my crystal glow." Llyr reached for his pockets. "I'll prove it."

He frowned, patting at his sides and desperately looking at the ground.

Mede arched a brow in disbelief. "Llyr, don't. Trying to alter the facts won't change anything." She stepped in a wide arch around him so he couldn't stop her. "I can't have this conversation with you. I need to help bury my fallen brother now."

"Of course, you're right. It was selfish of me to say anything. We must honor Cynan." Llyr looked desperate to say more but didn't. She turned her back on him to join the others.

Mede paused, listening for his footsteps. "Are you coming? We are in enemy territory right now."

Mede hoped the grief she felt over Cynan would hide her feelings for Llyr so that no one would detect the full depths of her agony. Today was not a good day. It might possibly be the worst day of her life.

She didn't need her crushed stone to tell her what she already knew. She loved Prince Llyr. Unfortunately, there was no clear map regarding how the crystals worked. It was possible her crystal would have glowed for Llyr, but his would not shine for her. Rare things did happen. Her very life was proof of that. Maybe she was unnatural and the gods did not want her reproducing. Maybe female dragons weren't supposed to exist. Dragons were hard. Women were supposed to be softer. Perhaps the balance she carried between woman and dragon was too challenging, too contradictory, too unstable, too impossible.

Llyr was not meant to be hers. Perhaps it was the whispering of the gods that had caused her to crush her stone as a young girl. They knew the heartache she'd feel when this moment came. But even their meddling could not save her from her own heartbroken fate. She would not be the reason the future Draig king did not have children, or a true mate, or true love.

The sacrifice was likely to kill her.

And how could she be so self-absorbed when Cynan was dead. She should have joined him in the cage. The scientists should have captured her instead. She wanted to turn around and kill the already-dead bastards.

"Mede?" Llyr whispered.

She realized she'd stopped walking. "I couldn't save him. I watched him die and I couldn't even touch his hand. I couldn't save him."

Llyr pulled her against his chest as she began to cry.

"I wanted to so badly," she wept, "but I couldn't save him."

CHAPTER 12

Llyr did not let Mede out of his sight as they made their way back through the marshes toward Draig land. Saben scouted ahead to make sure the path was clear. Arthur and Dylan moved through the trees on either side of the group. No one spoke.

Llyr again reached for his pocket. His crystal was gone. As they moved, he tried to find it on the ground, but there was no way of knowing how or when it had disappeared. When he'd made the decision to follow his friends, he had been focused only on tracking them and helping to ensure everyone was brought home safely. He couldn't even recall the exact path he'd taken, only that it had circled close to Lord Myrddin's home. For all he knew, his crystal was lost in marsh water and residing as bedding for a givre nest.

Today was not the day to convince Mede of his love. He had no proof. The grief of their loss was too fresh.

It seemed a long time before they crossed back into Draig territory.

Saben stopped near the border. "I'll see to Cynan's tent."

"I will help," Arthur answered.

"He has a brother who lives in the high mountains." Dylan looked to Llyr. "He needs to be told."

"I'm going to the mountains," Mede said. "I know the area. I was with him at the end. I should be the one to tell Cynan's brother that he died a hero."

"I'll come with you," Llyr said.

Mede looked at him and shook her head in denial. "No. You and Rolant should report to the king. Cynan's name needs to be honored. It's up to you to find out if the Var were responsible for bringing the scientists to our planet."

"She is right," Rolant agreed. "I'll go to the communications tower. We need to monitor space ships in our sky. Someone was coming to pick them up. You need to tell our parents what happened and then we all need to sit down and figure out what the Var are up to."

Llyr knew they were right. He didn't want Mede out of his sight, but at least the high mountain would take her far from the borders. There she would be safe. "Fine, but give me a moment alone with Lady Mede."

Rolant and Dylan left them alone.

"When you are done, I want you to go home and stay there until the Breeding Ceremony." Llyr couldn't resist touching her. He pulled her into his arms. "I need to know you are safe. It's the only way I can concentrate on doing what I must."

"I can take care of myself." She leaned back to touch the dormant crystal on his neck. "And you should focus on finding your mate."

"Mede," Llyr paused as he heard his brother talking to Dylan. This was not the time to explain. "It's a royal order. Go home after you speak to Cynan's brother. And you can't tell anyone how Cynan died. We can't cause panic. Just say he was a hero and acted with honor."

She glared at him and forced him to let her go with a hard push.

"Dylan," Llyr called. "She's ready."

"You can't order me, prince," she whispered.

"I just did," he stated. "Don't dishonor your family name by disobeying a royal decree." The last time he'd ordered her, he was going against the king's directive that all Dead Dragons in the area must go and fight. Now there was no such conflict and she would have to listen to him.

Dylan appeared with Rolant. He nodded at Mede and turned toward the mountains. She gave Llyr one last hard look before saying to Dylan, "I know where wild berries grow on the way if you're hungry."

"I don't really feel like eating," Dylan said.

"Neither do I." Mede did not look back. Llyr watched to see if she would.

"We have to go," Rolant said. "She will be fine. She's heading away from the Var."

"The Var king asked about her." Llyr couldn't keep his fear inside. "That is what our father wanted to tell me. The Var king asked to attend our wedding festival."

"Why would the Var king want to come to our Breeding Festival?" Rolant's entire body became stiff. As if coming to his own conclusion, he looked at where Mede had disappeared, and then back at his brother. "No. He couldn't think to marry—"

"Go to the communications tower and then meet me in the royal office." Llyr thought of his parents. "You can help me explain why I defied them and went after Mede. Or perhaps we should say I went after the Dead Dragons and not mention Mede? Mother will listen to you, and if you convince her, she will take care of our father."

Rolant gave a small, tired laugh. "Yeah,

brother, I will bail you out of trouble with our parents."

DRAIG PALACE'S Royal Office

"Mede carried herself like a true queen." Rolant eyed Llyr before focusing his attention on their parents. "She showed compassion when she sat with Cynar until his end. She was fierce as she led the Dead Dragons into battle to avenge that death. She was decisive when it came to dealing with the laboratory. And her commitment to her brother dragons runs deep."

They sat in the king's private office around a fireplace. Four chairs were situated in front of the fire around a table the queen had built with her own hands. The king and queen were upset by Llyr's departure into the Var forest to fight when there was no war.

For a moment, no one spoke. Then, suddenly, Queen Lorna sat up straighter and directed herself to her eldest son. "Rolant said she carries herself like a queen. She makes your crystal glow? She is the one?"

And there it was, Rolant's subtle touch with their mother. He always had a way of phrasing things so she'd be receptive to them. Rolant let a half smile curl briefly on the side of his mouth as Queen Lorna took the clue.

"Yes." Llyr nodded once.

"She is the reason you put yourself in unnecessary danger?" The queen had always told her sons there was no dishonor in hard work or hard choices. It had been her hard choice after her mother died to come to Qurilixen to marry a stranger, and the gods had rewarded her for that bravery with a good husband. Though, back then, there had been no contract with a bridal procurement ship, just personal advertisements in magazine chips.

"I came at your summons and, when you were done with me, I made the hard choice to defy standing tradition and join the Dead Dragons."

"When you discovered the Var king was inquiring about her, you went to protect her because you love her." The queen gave him a soft smile.

Llyr nodded. "Punish me if you must, but Cynan was my brother and Mede is my heart. I had to go."

"There will be no punishment for that," Queen Lorna said with a stern look at her husband, as if to dare him to disagree with her. He didn't.

"If she is to be my daughter, then why is she not here to meet us?" the king asked.

"Cynan has a brother who lives in the high mountains. She's gone to inform him of the death. I sent Dylan to escort her." Llyr tried not to let his worry show. He wanted to go after her, but knew that after his decree sending her home, she might not want to see him. "I figured she'd be safer there, away from the borders. The other Dead Dragons have been ordered to make camp near her home for protection. They do not know the full threat and they did not ask for details, but they will keep her safe."

"Have you learned more about why King Auguste is interested in Mede?" Rolant asked, before adding, "The Var king has not remarried. You don't think…?"

Llyr stiffened as he awaited his father's answer. Mede was his and Llyr wasn't going to let King Auguste near her.

"By all indications, his first wife was a full mate. He will not take another," King Tarec stated.

"Don't they half mate?" Rolant asked.

"Not after a full. They might take lovers, but I don't see the Var king going so far as to insult us by trying to make our one female dragon his mistress," Queen Lorna said.

"Don't you?" the king asked, clearly not as charitable in his opinion of the cat-shifters.

"What about the Var prince?" Rolant asked. "Does the king seek to marry off his son?"

"I think war is the more likely scenario here," the king stated. "The rumors of King Auguste's excessive drinking and erratic behavior have reached even my ears. It's no secret that Lord Myrddin and the other house nobles hate our kind. I pay a man well for information and it has come to my attention that Myrddin has been seen at the palace more and more over the last several years. With the Var presence near our borders and Cynan's murder, it can only be assumed they plan use Lady Medellyn as an excuse to get near the Breeding Festival. I am officially denying the request and increasing soldier patrols that night."

Rolant gave Llyr a guilty look, before saying, "Should we cancel the ceremony this year? Or at least move it?"

"The ceremony is sacred. It will take place and it will happen on sacred ground. I will not cower before the Var threat." King Tared lifted his jaw proudly.

"Even if the Var intentions are honorable, the fates have already decided that the lady is meant for your son," the queen said to her husband. "There is no reason for the Var to be there. You make the right decision."

"The Var and Draig should not mingle,"

Rolant said. "It is all we can do to coexist on the same planet."

"Llyr?" The queen straightened and gave him a worried look. "Where is your crystal?"

"Lost," Llyr admitted. He'd given Gildas' necklace back now that the man had recovered. It had been a stupid idea, one he never should have done. Now his own crystal was lost in the Var forest and he had no way of proving his love to Mede. "When we went after the scientists, I must have lost it. I looked for it but it's gone."

"But without it you cannot be married." The queen looked at her husband. "Can he?"

"It's no matter. It glowed. You both saw it. I will take the words of a Dead Dragon and my son at the ceremony. You will be married." The king reached his hand to his wife and she took it without hesitancy. "We are blessed early this year, my lady."

She nodded but still looked worried. "The gods smile on our family."

Llyr understood his mother's concern over his future. Tradition said Mede had to break his crystal at the ceremony to cement their bond. If that didn't happen, would they be able to truly mate? He wanted to believe what he felt for her was enough, but how could he know? Then there was the fact she'd never seen the crystal glow. Would she believe him if he tried to explain again? Would her father tell her? Surely she would believe her father. A small part of him wished she'd just trust what she felt and agree to marry him—crystal magic be damned.

VAR TERRITORY, Shadowed Marshes

"What are we doing out here?" Attor frowned at Myrddin. "I know you didn't summons me from my palace to wander the forest. I have no desire to commune with nature."

Unless her name is Mede and she's naked in my bed, he added silently. *I would like to commune with that nature.*

The breeze shifted and a horrible smell accosted him. He wrinkled his nose. "What is that rot? Did you bring me to show me dead animals?"

"Stop whining like a woman," Myrddin scolded. "I warned you I'd beat you if you became weak like your father. We're almost there."

It was rotting corpses Myrddin brought him to look at, only they weren't animals. Four dead humanoids lay on the ground, their bodies mangled with claw marks. Whoever had attacked them had made a big mess of things. Entrails were strewn over the forest floor. Body parts were flung here and there like morbid decoration.

Attor shrugged. "So you had some fun with the

aliens. I don't recognize them as palace guests if that's your worry—though it is hard to tell exactly what they looked like before all that damage. The only woman missing is that Syog you chased into the woods. Her traveling party hasn't seen her and they keep hassling me about her."

"The Syog? I know nothing about that," Myrddin said. "She probably ran off on one of the departing ships. The last I saw her she was on her hands and knees begging me."

Attor really couldn't care less about the dead people in his forest, or the Syog whore who'd let herself get captured by Myrddin. He waved his hand at the slaughtered aliens. "Have your guards burn them and be done with it. I'm not helping to clean this up."

"I brought you here to show you why we need to go to war with the Draig," Myrddin said. "These scientists were mine. I paid them to work on a top-secret project in my cave laboratory."

"You have a cave laboratory?" Attor asked.

"Not any more. The Draig destroyed it. You yourself saw the dragon woman in Var territory, running around like she had a right to be here. She's not the only one. The Draig have been crossing into our borders for some time."

"Skin a cat," Attor mumbled, remembering Mede's game.

"What?"

"They call their game skinning a cat," Attor said with much authority, as if he had knowledge way beyond Myrddin when it came to political matters. "They cross our borders to harass the marsh farmers for their fur."

"You call this a game?" Myrddin gestured angrily at the bodies. "This is an insult to not only my house, but yours, prince."

"What was your project?" Attor inquired. "Does my father know?"

"The king? That drunken lout is too busy pretending to be ruler while the rest of us protect this country. He is an old fool and I wouldn't ask his permission to squat in a forest, let alone protect your birthright, son. Someone has to protect the Var and you."

Attor stepped through the bodies to study them more closely. They had been torn with claws or talons, that much was evident. "What were they doing for you?"

"Making a weapon that could rid the planet of Draig once and for all. It would poison them and leave us unharmed. Only we would have the antidote. Those dragons who took their rightfully subservient place would receive the cure. Those who didn't would die." Myrddin looked very proud of his idea. "It was to be a gift at your coronation, to use as you saw fit. Only the Draigs trespassing ruined it. Look what they did. They killed my scientists before they had a chance to finish their work. They destroyed my lab, burying it under rubble. They're nothing but a bunch of animals."

"Careful," Attor said. "I am to marry one."

"I understand the necessity of your idea," Myrddin asserted, though he didn't seem to enjoy the thought. "Why not take a half mate figurehead wife, especially now that my plan is ruined. If she becomes burdensome, there are ways to rid yourself of an unwanted woman when she no longer serves a purpose."

Attor didn't want to think about killing Mede. He'd imagined their relationship in his head and it was going to be perfect. "These could be claw or talon made. How do you know it was the Draig?"

"I found this." Myrddin reached into his satchel and pulled out a dragon crystal. He tossed the necklace at Attor. "They never take those off unless it's to break them during a ceremony. One must have been pulled off during the slaughter."

Attor turned the stone between his fingers before tossing it up and catching it in a closed fist. "This rock will come in handy. Thank you."

Myrddin gave a hard sigh. "I didn't bring you here for a rock. I brought you to show you the need for war."

"My father does not want war. My father barely wants to leave his palace. I have to wait my turn. What do you want me to do?" Attor growled. "Kill the king?"

"No, no, you mustn't," Myrddin said slowly, as if he himself didn't believe his own halfhearted protest.

"I won't kill my father," Attor stated.

"Of course, prince. It would not do to start your reign under such a stain, even if the house nobles would support your ascension."

"Just so we are clear." Attor was bored with the conversation. "I'll talk to my father about the Draig entering our territory. In the meantime have your men patrol the borderlands."

He had no intention of speaking to his father about Myrddin's concerns, or anything else for that matter. He had already asked the king for help securing his bride and did not want to risk him changing his mind. Avoidance seemed to be the best plan where King Auguste was concerned.

"It's already done." Myrddin's smile was odd, but Attor wasn't interested in reading into it.

"I'm going back to the palace." Attor wrinkled his nose in disgust as he strode away from the scene. "Have your men burn this, and next time, skip the trip into the forest to see corpses. Just tell me what you need to tell me."

DRAIG NORTHERN MOUNTAINS, Medellyn's Family Home

"Medellyn, you have to get out of bed." Grace laid her hand over her daughter's head. "Come eat."

"I'm not hungry," Mede said into her pillow, not looking at her mother. She didn't want the gentlewoman to see her red eyes and know she'd been up crying again.

"What has happened to my headstrong daughter?" Grace asked, stroking her hair. "Why won't you talk about how Cynan died? I don't understand how you were unable to bring him home to his family. One can only conclude that the result was an image I don't want in my daughter's memory. Talking about it will help. Share your burden."

Mede thought of the black trails coming from

Cynan's eyes. They invaded her nightmares, showing up on every face in her dreams. As badly as she wanted to be able to bring his body home to his brother, they couldn't risk spreading the disease. All they could do was lock it away and pray to the gods that the secret died with the scientists. Dylan seemed fairly confident from reading the files that it was only contagious by direct contact. When the bodies decayed the disease should dry up. Since, out of all of the Dead Dragons, he had the most scientific knowledge, they had to trust in his assessment.

Mede could not put the image of Cynan's last moments into her mother's delicate mind. Actually, she couldn't tell anyone. Llyr had decided it was best not to panic the population with the idea of disease. Such panic would lead to suspicions and suspicions would lead to planetary war. They had no evidence to accuse Lord Myrddin or the Var people. All they had was a bad feeling deep in their guts that the time of peace was again coming to an end. War equaled death, and none of them wanted that. Things had been going so well. Why would the Var king want to change that?

"Why won't you answer me?" Grace whispered.

"It's the burden of secrets, mother," Mede answered. She finally looked up. "I can't say by royal decree."

Grace gave her a sympathetic smile and nodded in understanding. "Just make sure you talk to someone, Medellyn. Don't trap the ugliness inside."

"How was your trip to see the medic? I should never have told you to ride a ceffyl." Mede had been feeling guilty about that for some time. "You never said."

"I sent a runner. Since there is no time limit on when I have to see the medic, he'll stop past whenever he's in the area." Grace chuckled. "You really didn't think you could out manipulate your mother, did you?"

Mede shook her head in denial. "I thought you persuaded, not manipulated. I should have known you'd come up with an alternative solution."

"Anything to avoid climbing on a ceffyl." Grace tilted her head in thought. "What about Prince Llyr? I am sure he would listen to your worries. He seems very fond of you."

"What makes you say that?" Mede guiltily thought about their time in the cave, making passionate love. Even now the thought of it made her want to find him and kiss him, to never stop kissing him. Then she remembered the reason she was home instead of hiding with her grief in the forest was because he'd ordered it. She did not appreciate being told what to do. "What have you heard?"

"Should I have heard something?" Her mother arched a brow.

"No," Mede said weakly, unable to make eye contact. "Did you say food? I think I might be hungry."

She wasn't, but her mother had some kind of weird hostess sickness where she had to feed people.

To her surprise, Grace grabbed her hand, not instantly getting up to make a tray of food. "Oh, Mede, please tell me. I'm dying for you to tell me."

"I can't. Royal decree."

"Not that. Prince Llyr. He's the one, isn't he? I saw the way he looked at you. He's your mate. A mother knows these things. A mother knows when a beau is interested in courting her daughter."

"I don't understand you sometimes," Mede said.

"When a dragon wants to swoop in and lay claim to his mate." Grace's tone dropped as if saying such things were crass and not to be overheard. "Do you need me to tell you about mating? Do you know how babies are created?"

"They're gifts from the gods," Mede answered wryly. "Magically put in our bellies like seeds planted at harvest."

Grace made a weak noise. "Well, I know that's what I told you when—"

"Mother, I'm teasing. Yes, I know." Mede did not want to go into further detail.

"Oh, thank goodness." Grace sighed with relief and then stiffened. "Oh, no, the ceffyls. My darling girl, no. That is not the way of things between husband and wife. Don't feel bad. We had this common misconception when farm girls were around bred horses."

Mede stared, willing the woman to stop talking. She could be a hundred years old and she was pretty sure she would never, ever, not even under threat of death, ever want to have a talk about sex with her mother.

"I'm sorry, but you're wrong. I don't make his crystal glow." She tried to keep a straight face, but her heart broke at the words and she gasped, pressing her hand to her chest. A tear slipped over her cheek. "Please, don't talk about it."

"Then the crystal is wrong," Grace stated matter-of-factly. "Your Victorian ancestors did not need a crystal to tell them these things. Maybe since you're a dragon female you need both crystals to make them work. Since you broke yours, his doesn't glow. I saw the way he looked at you. It's the same way your father looks at me. It's the same way all these Draig men look at their wives. That man would jump off a cliff to make you happy. He'd run through fire, cut off his own hand, take over the entire universe if you asked it of him. I know you think I'm a silly woman with silly ideas, but I know love when I see it. That man loves you. And by the pain you're now feeling, I suspect you love him."

"Do you really think it's because we don't have both crystals?" Mede wanted to hope, but she worried that Grace's desire to see her daughter wed was tainting her judgment.

"Perhaps. Or perhaps you have to wait for the Breeding Ceremony for it to work. Or the gods are mad about you breaking your stone early and are toying with you." Grace took her daughter's hands and pulled them to rest above her heartbeat. "You don't need magic to tell you what your heart knows. When you close your eyes, who do you feel? Who do you think of? Who do you want to be with? That is your answer. You don't need me, or a crystal, or the gods to tell you who to love. You know who you love, Medellyn. It's as simple and as complicated as that."

"I don't know what I feel," she admitted. Another tear slid over her cheek. "I'm scared of being married. I never wanted marriage. I don't want to belong to somebody. I want to *be* somebody. I have fought my entire life to be as good, if not better, than any male dragon on this planet. I'm stronger and faster, and I work harder than they do. How can I give that up to be a wife?"

Grace did not pretend to be insulted by the honesty. She sighed, caressing her daughter's cheek and swiping the tear away with her thumb. "If you truly want to be as good as any of the male dragons on this planet, then you must accept love as they do. That is the one dragon trait you deny. They all know they are to marry and mate forever. Just as you are to someday marry. Marriage will not change who you are, Medellyn. It enhances you. And, if you choose Prince Llyr, you will not belong to a man. You will lead a nation. You are somebody, my fierce daughter. You will always be somebody. Marriage and motherhood will only add to the fullness of your life. No one can take away who you are unless you let them."

"And what if it's not meant to be? What if I go to the ceremony and his crystal glows for someone else? I can't watch that."

"If Llyr is not your prince, then another man will be at another time." Grace pulled her into her arms and held her tightly. "Then you do what everyone does after life gives you a bad turn. You come home. No matter what happens, you can always come home."

"Llyr is just..." Mede gritted her teeth, thinking

of their last encounter. "He's just so frustrating. He always tries to tell me what to do, or protect me, or—"

Grace chuckled and released her.

Mede frowned. "Don't laugh."

"Don't look at me like that," Grace said. "I laugh because I feel sorry for any man who tries to order you around. I imagine you try to protect him as much as he tries to protect you. A little friction in a relationship is part of the fun of it. Keeps things from getting boring."

"You and father never have friction."

Grace laughed harder, her entire body shaking as she swayed back. "Oh, not that you have seen. I would never argue with your father in front of you. That man can infuriate me like no other. We have mellowed with age and found a rhythm that works for us, but when we first married I wanted to drown him in a lake one moment, throw his muddy shoes at him the next, and then he'd do something incredibly endearing and I'd forget why I was irritated."

"Father? Endearing?" Mede loved the man, but he didn't really seem the romantic type.

"He once covered the entire house with solarflower petals," Grace said.

"That was him?" Mede's eyes widened in shock. "I remember that. I was, what, six years old?

I thought you did that as some kind of strange cleaning ritual."

"He wanted to make me smile. I thought I was pregnant again and it turned out to be nothing… again. The doctor checked me, told me I couldn't have more children, and I was so sad that I couldn't give him a larger family like other Draig wives. And do you know what he told me? He said I had already given him the rarest of solarflowers with a daughter and he didn't need sons. He had me and he had you and that made his life complete."

"Why didn't you ever tell me this?"

"You were a child and one does not tell a child about adult things. But I've seen you grow so much, Mede. I see a maturity in you that was lacking even two months ago. Maybe it was what happened to Cynan. Maybe it's Llyr." Grace stood and pulled Mede to her feet. She sighed and looked at an exterior wall as if she could see through it. "Now, daughter, what am I to do with the army of men on our lawn? They refuse to leave by order of the prince, and they sing songs not fit for a lady's ears."

Mede laughed, unable to help it. The Dead Dragons had made their camp close to her home, not the lawn like her mother claimed, but they were close enough to be heard shouting in the early hours of the morning. "I think the prince wanted them away from the borders after Cynan's death, so he ordered them here with me to keep them from seeking revenge."

"So the death has something to do with the borderlands?" Grace asked, perceptively.

"Would you like me to speak to them and send them away?" Mede started to stand.

"No." Grace placed a firm hand on her shoulder. "Let's feed you. There is food in the kitchen. You eat something. I'll speak to them. I know how to handle dragons."

Minutes later, Mede found herself standing in the doorway to her home, watching in awe as her mother gently scolded the hardened warrior men about their lack of harmony when drinking, their dusty boots and their unwashed hands. By the time she was finished, they were offering to cut her a woodpile and eating dainty sweet biscuits off a tray. Not once did her mother threaten violence on them or raise her voice to be heard.

"Perhaps I underestimated the lady's approach," Mede said when Grace returned with an empty tray.

"You will be amazed what men will do for food," Grace answered. "Whenever I want your father to do something I make his favorite dish. He still hasn't caught on."

"I think your skills go beyond serving sugared

biscuits." Mede took the empty tray. "You didn't let them have all of them, did you?"

"Of course not. I set aside the two biggest for you." Grace gestured to the kitchen. "Why don't you put that tray on the counter, grab the biscuits, and then would you mind coming to the back room with me to help me with something?"

"Of course, anything. I will be right there." Mede was already on her way to the kitchen thinking of the treat. "I still can't believe you got them to do what you wanted with food." Mede chuckled. "Men are such simple creatures to be manipulated so easily. It makes me glad I'm a woman and too smart to fall for such tricks."

"Yes, dear," Grace answered with a small laugh. She waited until Mede came back out holding a biscuit in each hand. Leading the way to the back room, she said, "I need you to try on the wedding undertunic gown. I had the hem altered. It was a bit long."

Mede paused in the middle of the living room and watched her mother disappear into the back room. Realizing she'd also been persuaded by the promise of food into agreeing to do *anything*, she grimaced. Under her breath, she muttered, "You're lucky these are really good." Defiantly shoving one into her mouth whole, she went to do what her mother wanted.

LLYR WANTED nothing more than to go to the mountains to see Mede. He knew she was safe, because he'd ordered the Dead Dragons to run reports to him as he camped with the Draig army near the borderlands. He was with a small group of warriors who had been called away from their homes, but they were trustworthy and brave. The king wanted the men prepared for the night of the festival and had entrusted Llyr to see to their assignments. The Dead Dragons needed time to grieve, so Llyr did not make them do this task.

The night of darkness was fast approaching. There was so much he wanted to say to Mede, but keeping her safe was a much more pressing matter. He sent men over the borders to check for signs of Var movement. They built perches in the trees near the festival grounds to better watch the festivities and the forest.

With his attention on every detail, Llyr worked for most of the day. Each evening, when the sky dimmed by small degrees, he sneaked away to a little stone temple overgrown with vines and vegetation, to lay prostrate on the hard stone ground before the gods.

The gods wouldn't care that nature had overtaken the small ruins. Time had actually added to the spiritual power of the place and enhanced his personal sacrifice. He begged the gods for their blessing, to forgive his loss of the crystal, to protect Mede from harm and to make her his wife. Only when he could barely keep his eyes open and his body was so stiff it hurt to move, did he allow himself to crawl off to find a few hours of sleep before doing it all again.

"WHAT DO you mean King Tared said no?" Attor demanded, as he stormed into his father's bedchamber. He threw the missive his father had redirected to him. The parchment landed on the man's bed.

King Auguste muttered incoherently, half-awake and half-dead drunk.

The dazed state gave Attor courage. "I asked you for one thing. One! Lady Medellyn is to be my wife. The gods were clear. I want her. I need her."

The king grumbled and launched a pillow in Attor's direction. He caught it in one hand and gripped it tightly. King Auguste turned his back to Attor in dismissal.

Attor stormed around the bed. "You are a useless king, a worthless father and a sorry excuse for a cat. The Var would be better off if you abdicated the throne." He hit him with the pillow, hard.

King Auguste growled and slashed a hand toward Attor. His eyes weren't even open all the way, as if his son was no real threat to be taken seriously. "Leave me, you ungrateful, entitled brat. What do you know about ruling the kingdom? The only thing you've accomplished in your miserable life is killing your mother!"

Rage burst out of Attor, causing him to shift uncontrollably. Claws gripped the pillow, clenching so forcefully he couldn't compel his own hands to open. He simply stood, shaking violently.

"Worthless," King Auguste muttered, moving to turn on the bed to again give Attor his back.

Attor lunged forward. He landed on the bed, stopping his father from dismissing him yet again. King Auguste floundered in surprise. Unable to release his hold, Attor used the pillow to smother the king's disgusting face. He wanted to erase the hateful words. He wanted to erase his childhood. He wanted to erase his father.

When King Auguste tried to fight back, Attor pressed his knees forward, locking the pillow down and pinning the king's arms at the same time. The king shifted, trying to slash at his son. Attor barely felt the cuts on his forearm before he captured the wrists. Rage kept him strong, stronger than he ever remembered feeling.

"You're a worthless father. You're a worthless father," he repeated, locked in position long after the man's weakening blows stopped.

Attor's breath came in harsh pants. His fists slowly unfurled and he released the pillow. He backed away, coming off the bed.

Not really thinking, he slid the pillow off the king's face. One of King Auguste's eyes looked at him through a narrow slit. The other was closed.

His hands shook and he glanced around the room. He shook the pillow of any indentation and shoved it beside his father's head. The body was still warm as he pushed the eyelid down to hide the accusing gaze. Numbly, he grabbed the letter from the floor and backed out of the room. "Yes, father, you sleep. Sleep."

DRAIG BREEDING FESTIVAL GROUNDS, Outside the Royal Palace

Music filtered over the festival grounds, the sound of *gitterns* filling the one night a year when the Draig people could marry. Llyr loved the strumming resonance of the four-stringed instruments. Bonfires had been lit, giant blazes that could surely be seen from space. The placement of the fires was to help guide the bridal procurement ship to where it needed to land, which it had done an hour before. A new bright green and pink logo had been painted on its hull that read, "GB" for Galaxy Brides. The ship had yet to open as it sat in a clearing on the hill. Though he understood the necessity of his father's trade with the procurement corporation, Llyr was not interested in the alien brides. He knew his fate.

He'd been coming to the festival for years with his parents, but this was his first year attending as a groom. Since he knew who he wanted to marry, he did not bother to go down to the receiving area with the other men. He didn't want to explain why his crystal was lost. For the moment, everyone could assume it was under his silken groom shirt.

The masked grooms mingled with the gathered crowd. As the one night a year came over the planet, stars shone from above. Spots of burning ash spit up from the bonfires, the red embers floating in the darkness. The thick leaves slumped on the colossal trees of the forest. Unlike the mountains, the trees by the palace were fat and overgrown. Roasting food, burning wood, sleeping foliage, they all mingled into a scent that was unique to this night and this place.

Once the ship's doors opened, the grooms would form a line. The alien women would walk by. Crystals would glow. Marriages would be set or disappointments felt.

Large pyramid-shaped tents had been assembled around the edges of the festival grounds for the lucky couples. Families decorated the tents with colorful banners and crests, as a symbol of familial blessing and well wishes. A torch had been lit near each tent's entrance and would burn throughout the night. Those not attending the ceremony as a groom showed their loud support by reveling around the fires—dancing, drinking and playing in celebration.

His parents were seated across the crowd from his location, presiding over the ceremony from their wooden thrones. He knew the king would be holding his wife's hand in his, as the queen whisperingly remembered how they met at their ceremony long ago.

Rolant stepped up onto the wooden platform that would later host a feast for the bridal candidates. Llyr stood on it to get a better view of the festival grounds. Handing his brother a goblet of mead, Rolant grinned. "She's here."

"You saw her?" Llyr asked, eagerly looking around the site. "Where? Is she dressed as a bride?"

"I saw her parents." Rolant took a drink from his goblet, finishing it off before handing it to a passing servant. "Lady Grace asked about you."

"What did she say?" Llyr didn't take a drink, so Rolant took the goblet from him and lifted it to his own lips. "Did she say Mede was here to marry me?"

Rolant chuckled. "She wanted to know where your tent was. Our father didn't have a tent set up for Mede since he's convinced the lady will be in yours with you tonight, so I'm guessing Lady Grace wanted to pin ribbons to it for luck. I would say that is a sign."

"Her father saw my glowing crystal when we delivered the ceffyls to the northern valley. He could have told his wife, and they both assumed." Llyr frowned in worry. "Mede might have other plans. She's hardheaded and makes her own decisions."

It was one of the things he loved about her, even as it frustrated him.

"Don't fear, brother. You've spent your time at the temple, praying to the gods, and denying your desire to see her again before tonight. I'm sure they saw your sacrifice."

Llyr would have lain on that hard temple stone for ten thousand years if it meant he'd be gifted with Mede in the end. He reached for his neck, as if this time the crystal would reappear to help him convince Mede of his love. "I shouldn't have tricked her."

"No, you probably shouldn't have," Rolant agreed. "But I can understand why you did. The lady would have run from you and hidden from the ceremony if she saw your crystal glow for her. You would not have lasted three minutes in her presence. I think you approached her the only way you could have—as a friend."

"I wrote her a note," Llyr admitted softly. "I wrote her fifty notes. I wanted to see how she was doing after Cynan's death."

"You did?" Rolant asked in surprise. "Did she answer?"

"I didn't send them. I couldn't risk the gods thinking my sacrifice halfhearted." Llyr frowned. "What if she thinks I do not care about her grief?"

"I am not sure Mede is the type of woman who would want people pointing out her grief." Rolant finished off his second goblet of mead and handed the empty cup to a servant. "Two more, please."

The servant nodded.

"She is not as tough as you make her sound. I think she merely hides her emotions well, like any warrior. It does not mean we do not feel." Llyr again searched the crowd. Where was she?

"Try to relax and enjoy the night. You have men posted all around the area. No one is getting by our guards. Mede is in the crowd. She is safe. I gave orders for Dylan to shadow her wherever she went, before they even left for the high mountains to see Cynan's brother. Dylan will not stop watching her until you tell him to."

Llyr relaxed at the news. "Thank you."

"You should put on your groom mask," Rolant said. "A bride is not supposed to see her husband's face before the acceptance."

Llyr had forgotten to put it on in his haste to find Mede in the crowd. He reached into his pocket and took out the silken mask. It matched the light blue of his tunic shirt. His white breeches had matching blue cross-lacing down each side of the leg. The cut of the clothing was very old-fashioned, but it was traditional groom attire. His people were hesitant to change their ways, especially since so many grooms had found happiness in such attire—as if changing the design of his pants would somehow taint a prospective marriage.

Thinking he needed all the luck he could get, Llyr tied the mask around his head. The silk encased his eyes from brow to nose, with holes that were just large enough to see through. The mask was a symbol of unwavering belief, choosing with the heart not the eyes. He heard his father once say it was from the days when grooms would cover themselves fully in a sheet and the brides would not see them before they chose by blind faith. Llyr wasn't sure how true the story was, or if it was just a tale passed down through generations.

Laughter punctuated the night. Llyr felt Mede but could not see her. The sensation of her washed over him, filling him with desire and longing. An invisible thread pierced his heart and sewed it to hers. Distance and time would not break such a bond. Even if she refused him, he would always love her. There was no one else. There had never been anyone else. Even when he'd been a young boy, he'd dreamed only of a shifter girl.

Not much scared the future king of the dragons, but the idea of not having Mede in his life terrified him. He held his breath, frantically searching for her, trying to follow his emotions.

His eyes caught sight of her near one of the nearby wedding tents, and he was able to breathe again. She wore the white bridal gown he'd seen her in at her home, the day she'd fallen into his arms. Even now he could feel her body against his.

The servant arrived with the goblets and Rolant reached to take both of them. He turned to hand one to his brother, but Llyr ignored him as he leapt off the wooden platform. The crowd parted to let him pass and he smiled at the sea of faces as he made his way to Mede. He had to see her. Whatever it took, he had to convince her she was meant to be his wife.

WHAT WAS SHE DOING HERE?

This was a mistake.

Was it a mistake?

Mede felt like a fool. People kept staring at her in the lacey bridal gown and smiling. They smiled a lot. She wasn't sure if they were laughing at how ridiculous she looked, or genuinely being nice. She'd give her dominant knife hand for a tunic shirt and some privacy.

Her mother had laced the restrictive bodice, tight but not as securely as before. Mede was still convinced that the corset was invented to prevent her from shifting and running away. How could she run if she couldn't fill her lungs with air? How could she run with so many lace and silk layers attacking her legs? The tip of her finger shifted into a talon and she was tempted to snag the corset string to loosen it. Maybe then her breasts wouldn't look so on display.

The gauzy brush against the back of her hand reminded her of how her mother had cried happy tears of joy when she'd put the veil bracelets on Mede's wrists. Mede retracted the talon and left the gown uncut. Nerves made it hard to swallow. Her dress made it hard to breathe. Her overactive thoughts made it hard to concentrate past the lightheadedness that took up residence in her brain.

What if Llyr's crystal still didn't glow?

What if she was meant to be heartbroken forever?

What if his feelings had changed since she'd last seen him?

What if this horrible ache inside her never went away?

Mede hadn't been nice to him the last they'd seen each other. She'd been distracted by grief and anger. She should have smiled at him. She should have said, *I love you, too.*

She should run. Running would be so much easier than facing her fears. Her body stiffened, begging her to shift and take to the forest, to find the familiar rhythm of feet against earth. Her mind forced her body to behave. Besides, she wasn't sure the corset would let her shift without breaking a couple of ribs.

"Mede?"

The whisper came from behind, startling her, and she nearly screamed. She closed her eyes. "Llyr."

She felt him step around her. Her breathing quickened, as did her heart. A hand touched her cheek. A shiver worked its way over her.

"It is good to see you," he said.

Mede opened her eyes. She started to smile, but stopped. Her gaze happened to be on his neck when she looked at him. He wore no necklace. How could that be? Had he found someone already?

"I should," she tried to speak but her throat closed. No one could be expected to live with the pain she felt in this moment. She waited, sure it was going to kill her. Somehow she remained standing. "I..."

"What?" The mask hid the upper part of his face, but that only caused her to focus on his piercing eyes and firm mouth. She remembered the feel of those lips on hers. She'd dreamed about his kisses each night, felt them in the hazy plateau between sleep and wake each morning.

"Congratulate you on..." She shook her head unable to say the words. "Go. I mean I should go."

"Mede, wait, please don't. I want to talk to you." Llyr reached for her arm, hesitated and then touched her gently.

"I know. I see many blessings are in order. You don't have to explain further. It's bad luck to talk until your bride takes off your mask, Prince Llyr." Mede wanted to rip the wedding gown from her body and run into the mountains. Surely if she went far enough she could end the pain in her chest. "You don't want to—"

"Then take it off," he said.

Mede made a small noise. "Don't tease me. I can see your crystal is gone."

"I lost it when we were in the Var forest. I guess the gods decided they want us to figure this out for ourselves without their guidance."

"I know you didn't lose it. I saw you wear it

home when we came back." She shook her head, wishing she could believe him. "Taking it off does not change the will of the gods."

"Forget the crystals. Forget the gods. Mede, I love you. I want you to be my queen. Not because you're the female dragon. I want you because you are you. I want you because I can think of nothing more pleasing in life than making you smile. I want you to be happy, and I want to be the cause of that happiness. I want to touch you and kiss you and be with you."

Mede heard someone laugh and turned to see Dylan grinning at them. He lifted his goblet, unashamedly watching and listening to what they said. Llyr lifted his hand and said, "Go away, Dylan. Find someone else to harass."

Dylan bowed, not losing his smile for one instant. "Yes, my prince, as you wish."

Taking Llyr's wrist, Mede pulled him away from the main gathering to a more private area behind the nearby tent where they could not be seen by the crowd.

"You really don't know how to be quiet, do you? It's bad luck for you to talk yet." Mede stood closer to him now that they had some privacy. The material of the veil swept behind her back, keeping her wrists tied together so she couldn't easily wrap her arms around him.

"I'll be quiet if you tell me you'll marry me." He cupped her face and leaned to kiss her mouth. Llyr moaned against her lips. "Say you'll be my bride. Say you'll have me forever."

Maybe she was crazy.

Somehow she didn't care.

"I'll have you, Llyr," she answered. "Forever."

"Llyr? Llyr are you back here? They need you so we can begin the ceremony," Rolant called. He came around the tent. Seeing Mede with her face in Llyr's hands, he grinned. "Greetings, Mede."

"Prince Rolant," she acknowledged, not bothering to hide her happiness.

"Llyr, the king and queen wait for you," Rolant said. "Unless you want me to tell them you're setting a poor example by kissing your bride behind the tents before the ceremony officially begins?"

"Ignore him," Llyr told Mede. "He can't handle his drink."

"Who said I was his bride?" Mede asked, wondering how Rolant knew what she herself had only just confirmed.

"You'd better be. I cannot stand my brother's pining for you. It's rather pathetic the way he carries on." Rolant surged forward and grabbed Llyr's arm. "Come, brother, there are other grooms waiting for marriage. The sooner you do this, the sooner you can come back here and get to the wedding night."

"Go," Mede urged. "I'll watch you from here."

"I don't want to leave you. Come with me."

"No. I don't want to be on stage. This gown has already brought me too much attention. You go. I'll wait."

"Perhaps you're right. I don't want anyone else trying to steal you away from me." Llyr kissed her again. He slid his tongue forward for a brief second before Rolant jerked him away. Llyr chuckled, letting his brother drag him. He faced Mede, stumbling backwards, and lifted his hand to his heart. "I love you."

Mede was about to say it back when Llyr was pulled out of her sight. Her heart pounded violently. She smiled in happiness.

"Gods, please don't strike us down if we defy you, but I can't live without him," she whispered. Mede passed behind a tent and then another, walking until she could get a clear view of the thrones. Llyr wasn't yet through the crowd and so the king and queen sat alone.

Her smile faltered. Queen. She would someday be queen. Mede stared at Queen Lorna, narrowing her eyes so that the distant face came into focus above the crowd. The woman looked as if she'd been born to the throne, regal and elegant. Just moments before Mede had wanted to rip out of her dress and run feral through the forest. How could she be queen?

Llyr and Rolant joined their parents. She looked at the people facing the royal family. How could she lead them? She was just a dragon from the mountains.

Panic filled her. She loved Llyr so much, but had she thought through what life would be like with him?

Llyr turned to the crowd and she focused on his face. A feeling of calm invaded her and she relaxed. Nothing would be as bad as life without him. She could do this.

"I found you."

At first, Mede didn't think the words were for her. She stood up on her toes, leaning to see over the heads that swayed into her field of vision.

"I knew we were meant to be together."

The words were closer. Mede frowned, turning around. She eyed the man before her. He was dressed in a tunic shirt and pants, both of the Var style. His blond hair was slicked back from his face. Somehow, the hairstyle made his features more severe. It took her a moment to place him.

"You're the man from the forest," she said, gesturing at his arm. "The one who gave me the fur."

"You remember me." He lifted his arm and traced his finger down a thin scar her cut had left. "I told you that you would be thinking of me since our time together."

Mede frowned, confused. She really hadn't thought about this man at all. Not since meeting Llyr. "I don't understand. What are you doing here?"

The man laughed. "As if you don't know already."

Her frown deepened and her body tensed in warning. "I don't know. You're trespassing. This is a sacred event. What is a Var royal guard doing at a Draig festival?"

The cat-shifter tossed back his head, laughing harder. "You worry about me trespassing? After the way we first met? Dragons hardly respect our borders. Do you really think your king could keep me from the ceremony?"

"What are you talking about? Why would a Var guard even want to be at this ceremony?" Mede glanced back. All eyes were still turned to King Tared. She heard the tone of the king's voice but could not concentrate on the words of his blessing.

"I'm hardly a mere palace guard," the man stated.

"Then who are you and what do you want?" Disgust filled her. She hated the cat-shifters. She knew it was wrong to hate a group of people for the actions of a few, but she couldn't help how she felt. She didn't need solid proof to know deep inside that Var hired the scientists. The death of Cynan was too new.

"I'm your groom. I've come to marry you."

Mede shook her head in denial. "I will never marry a cat. I'm to marry Prince Llyr. It's already been settled."

"So that is why King Tared denied my request to come tonight? He wanted you for his son. But don't worry. I can protect you. I am heir prince to the Var throne. I have come to claim you as my wife and take you to your new home. So you see, you do not have to fear for my life if you come with me. The dragon king cannot hurt me."

Mede wondered if the cat-shifter had always had that wild look in his eyes. The small kindness he'd shown in giving her the fur kept her from yelling out. "That's not how this works. There are customs. Laws. I'm to marry Prince—"

"Here." The Var man tossed a small object in her direction. On reflex she caught it against her body. The veil hindered her movement and she cupped it to her stomach. "Break it and let's go. I can't stay long."

"Who do you think you are coming here to make decrees?" She noticed a soft glow and looked down. The crystal she held shone in the dark night. She gasped, dropping it as if burned. "It can't be."

"I knew it. I knew you were meant for me." The glow excited the Var prince and he came for her. She stumbled back, stunned. "Now you have seen our fate—"

"Who do you think you are?" she repeated more forcefully.

"Prince Attor, future King of Qurilixen."

"There is no King of Qurilixen, only Var and Draig." Why was the crystal he threw at her glowing? She was in love with Llyr, not this man. Why would the gods betroth her to a Var? And the Var prince? "I don't understand. Are we to make peace? Does our marriage somehow stop a war? I can't...I don't..."

Why would the gods expect this sacrifice?

"Break the stone and let us go back to my palace." Prince Attor grew progressively more irritated with her. His smile faded and she saw his jaw clench.

"How did you get a stone?" The evidence of this man's claim was staring up at her, but she didn't want to believe it. Who did he hurt to get it? "Var don't have stones."

"What does it matter?" Attor leaned down, picked it up and then reached forward to forcefully hook the strand of leather around her neck.

The stone glowed brighter when it touched her skin.

If this was a sign from the gods then why did she want to scream for help and run for Llyr? "I don't…" She shook her head in denial. "No. I'm not going anywhere with you. You did me a favor once, which is the only reason I'm not screaming for a guard right now."

In irritation, Attor reached for her arm and grabbed it. "I don't have time for this. We have to go."

"Unhand me." She jerked but her feet caught in the skirts of the wedding gown and she tripped. A heavy fist hit her from behind and she stumbled forward, dazed. Her vision blurred as she fought to right herself. She opened her mouth to scream. Another smack sent her flying to the ground. Her head bounced up and then there was nothing but blackness.

CHAPTER 15

"FOR THOSE OF you blessed with a bride, it will be one of the *hardest* nights of your life." King Tared's voice boomed over the crowd. The men cheered in excitement and the teasing started. Council elders had joined the royal family on the stage to show support.

The queen gave her husband a properly exasperated look but did not interrupt. She leaned to whisper to Llyr, "Every year he does this."

"Every year you let him drink before his speech," Llyr whispered back.

"We are strong!" the king yelled, pumping his fist up into the air.

"We are strong!" Llyr yelled with the crowd as they answered the king's cry.

"We are brave!" King Tared prompted.

"We are brave!" Llyr put his fist in the air as they returned the king's chant. He grinned at his brother who shook one of the more stoic council elders by the arm. The older shifter tolerated the younger prince's playfulness.

"We are Draig!" everyone yelled in unison before cheering erupted over the field.

Llyr patted his father's shoulder as the king resumed his place on the throne. He laughed as the rowdy crowd didn't settle.

The queen let them have their moment before she moved to where her husband had been standing. She stood graciously, smiling at their people as she waited for them to calm. Seeing her, the onlookers quieted in respect.

"My wonderful people," the queen said, not quite as loudly as her husband, but with dragon-shifter hearing they would be able to make out her words just fine. "Many blessings on you and many blessings on this night. As once an offworld bride coming to your planet, you welcomed me. I ask that you welcome the women who come tonight. Some will be lucky enough to stay. Treat them well, my dragons, respect them, and the gods will smile on you as I smile upon you now."

"To our queen!" a voice from the crowd yelled.

"To our queen! To our queen!" the chanting started.

Queen Lorna took a seat next to her husband. The king lifted her hand and brought it to his lips. Llyr saw his father mouth, "To my queen." His mother touched the king's face and leaned her forehead lovingly to his.

Llyr glanced to where he'd last seen Mede watching him from between two tents. The crowd shifted and moved as the visiting spaceship began to open. Grooms went to line up to greet the brides. Their excitement was palpable.

"Go." The queen had turned to look at him. "Find your bride. We won't expect to see you until the morning."

Llyr leaned to kiss her cheek. He felt Rolant slapping him on the back.

Excited, he jumped off the platform into the crowd. His progress was slow as he tried to make his way to where he'd last seen Mede. Everyone he passed wanted to wish him luck or tease him about his upcoming night. He took their attentions in good-natured stride, but all he really wanted to do was go back to kissing his bride.

"Sacred cats, be careful!" Attor commanded Myrddin. "I would like her conscious when I take her to my bed tonight."

"She was about to alert the others." Myrddin hefted Mede over his shoulder and hurried for the nearby tree. "You were taking too long. We have to get back before your father knows we're missing."

"I'm not scared of my father," Attor stated. "And I'm not scared of these animals."

Myrddin nodded with pride. "Even so, we should get back. We cannot fight the entire crowd with an army of two."

"Do you see how her stone glows?" Attor dropped behind Myrddin to take the crystal from Medellyn's neck to show the man. "The gods speak to me—what? Where did it go?"

"Come, prince, we must hurry," Myrddin insisted, walking faster.

"We are strong!" the crowd cheered. Attor glanced toward the Draig and grimaced.

Attor looked around at the ground. "You must have dropped it. I need to find—"

"You don't need a stupid Draig custom." The man turned and strode back to where Attor stood. "All you need to do is decree she is your half mate. You're the prince. No one will dispute it. I'll witness. The only one who can undo your claim is the king and he's probably passed out drunk by now. If she protests and doesn't behave, we'll lock her in my dungeon until she does."

Attor didn't like being ordered around. His eyes narrowed. "Stop talking and move."

Myrddin blinked in surprise at the hard tone.

"We are brave!"

"We are Draig!"

"You are imbeciles," Myrddin muttered under his breath, dismissing the dragons at real threats.

Attor brushed past him. "Let's go while they're distracted by this nonsense."

LLYR'S SMILE faded as he finally made it across the field to the tents. Mede was not there. He glanced around, wondering where she could have gone. Did she go to their wedding tent? She said she'd wait for him.

This was not right. A strange feeling of foreboding came over him. She would not leave him, not after she said she'd marry him. Mede was not some flighty creature who changed her mind on a whim. If she said something she meant it. That could only mean something had happened to her. He closed his eyes, trying to feel her. The connection between them had tried to form, but the ceremony wasn't complete. They weren't truly mated, and until that happened he would not hear her call inside his mind.

Instead of once again trying to cross through the thick crowd to get to his tent on the far side of the grounds to look for her, he decided to run the long way around the outside circle of wedding tents where it was less crowded. A servant passed him, nodding happily and wishing him luck. Llyr automatically smiled and answered without really hearing what he said.

As he came around the tent, he whispered, "Gods, help me. We're so close to joining. Let me feel her. Let me find her."

His boot caught on a loose stone and he nearly tripped. He glanced down, intent on running. A glow caught his attention. Llyr reached for the abandoned crystal. The glow brightened when he touched it. The familiar shape was as known to him as his own hand, for he'd had it almost as long.

My crystal?

He glanced around. How did his crystal come to be where Mede had been standing when last he'd seen her?

The realization hit him like a fist to the gut. He'd lost the stone in the Var forest.

"Mede," he whispered.

If she was in his tent, she was safe. But if his stone was a sign from the gods, it meant that King Auguste had ignored their denial of his request, and sent men to capture Llyr's bride. They must have slipped in while the guards were distracted by the king's speech. As much as he wanted to find the men and shake them from their tree perches for the inattentiveness, he knew finding Mede and getting her home safely was more important.

He scanned the ground for tracks. Boot prints led into the trees.

"Prince Llyr, what are you doing? Shouldn't you be in the receiving line with the others?"

Llyr looked up. He pulled the mask off his face and tucked it into his waistband. "Saben, come, help me."

The Dead Dragon instantly dropped his goblet on the ground and joined the prince.

"I think the Var have taken my bride." Llyr pointed to the tracks.

Saben looked at the glowing crystal Llyr held and then at the ground. "Should I alert the guards?" He made a move as if to go.

"No, I don't want them to realize we are on to them," Llyr said. "If we raise an alarm they'll know something is up and we'll cause a panic in the crowd. It will be chaos. You're the best tracker. Help me find her quietly."

"But if the Var attack—"

"Trust me, Saben. They came for Mede. King Auguste wants her. He already tried to take her through diplomatic channels. We refused, so he's come to take her by force."

"That is why you sent us to guard her," Saben said, again looking at the glowing stone in Llyr's hand. "Gods' bones. Are you saying Mede is your bride? How did we not know this?"

"Saben," Llyr insisted sternly getting the man to focus.

Saben turned his attention to the ground and led the way from the tents to the trees. Once they were concealed, they both shifted to full dragon to better see in the dark.

"I smell cat," Saben whispered. "It's faint."

"What about Mede? Is there any sign of her?" Fear tried to creep in and Llyr endeavored to draw comfort from his stone. Surely the gods were with him. They would find her. They had to find her.

"I only see two tracks. They look too big to be Lady Mede."

"They have her. I know it." Llyr slipped his necklace over his head where it belonged.

Saben did not question the claim. "They did not try to hide their path. It could be a trap."

"Or they hurry to escape before Mede is discovered missing," Llyr answered.

Saben picked up the pace. Llyr practically felt the man's tension. After Cynan, they all resented the Var—though they had no solid proof of the

Var involvement. The fact King Auguste had dared to send men over the border to kidnap one of their women only turned resentment to rage.

Saben suddenly stopped and glanced around. Llyr could see for himself that two tracks ended in a struggle of some sort and then became one. They both instantly looked up to the trees. A sickening cat-like *rawr* sounded as a flash of paws showed from above. Llyr leapt, grabbing an ankle and pulling to throw the dark-furred shifter off course.

"That way. Find her!" Saben pointed that Llyr should follow the tracks before he jumped onto their attacker.

Llyr hurried through the forest. The sounds of a fight came from behind him. His heart pounded violently now that his suspicions had been confirmed. The Var were in their forest.

He ran farther from the ceremony into the trees. It was too late to turn back. He had to go after her alone.

CHAPTER 16

MEDE JERKED HERSELF AWAKE. Something bound her hands and she instantly fought to be free of the ties. Her back scraped against a grainy texture. It took her eyes a while longer to focus in the dark, and she had to blink several times to clear her head.

She was bound to a tree with what felt like her wedding veil. Though she tried to be brave, a wave of fear washed over her and she began to shake. Her breath came in uneven pants as she forced herself to focus. Trees. She was tied to a tree. They weren't large like the forest near the palace, nor skinny like the forests near her home. She was in the borderlands. Where exactly was impossible to tell. With no landmarks, she could be anywhere along a several mile stretch.

She smelled the faint odor of rot. The marshes? That narrowed it down some. If she ran away from that smell she might make it back to familiar terrain—unless of course she ran southeast, which would drive her deeper into Var territory.

She had no doubt she was on the wrong side of the border. Prince Attor would have taken her somewhere he felt safe.

Prince Attor. The man who'd kissed her in the forest was the Var prince? By his arrogant bearing and speech, she could believe he was royalty. He also seemed slightly insane, talking about how they were meant to be married, as if that insignificant moment meant more than it did. All their meeting had meant to her was an end to her initiation period. Had she not found Attor, she would have taken fur from the marsh farmer. She didn't care if the man handed her fifty thousand glowing crystals, she was never going to marry him. She loved Llyr. No stupid rock was going to tell her what to do.

Llyr. Would he think she'd run off on him? Would he know to look for her? It would take him a long time to search the crowd. It might be morning before anyone realized she was gone. Thinking of the drinking, she frowned. It might be late, late morning before anyone realized she had gone.

"Good. You're awake."

Mede stiffened, forcing the shaking fear inside

her to stop as she looked at Prince Attor. "What are you doing? Kidnapping a Draig citizen is an act of war. Do you really want to start the bloodshed between our people again?"

"Kidnapping?" Attor gave a dark laugh and came more into view. She stiffened. His tunic shirt was splattered with blood. "I claim you, Lady Medellyn as my first half mate. You cannot kidnap a wife."

Mede gasped. "I don't accept. I'm to be married elsewhere tonight. The promises have already been spoken. The gods have—"

"No one asked you!" Attor roared. Mede jerked back at the uncontrolled anger on his face. "Welcome to the Var throne, my wife."

Attor came close and she tried to burrow her body into the unyielding tree bark. His hot breath fanned over her neck. She tried to kick, but her feet were secured. He ignored the defiance. His eyes dipped down to where the bodice pushed up her breasts. When he lifted his hand, she smelled blood. She tried not to look at him, but his face pressed insistently near hers as if to force her to meet his gaze. A single claw touched the top mound of her breast, tracing the hemline of her bodice.

"Our children will be exquisite, my wife," he whispered. "Half cat, half dragon, our stunning genetics—such powerful sons. I will be known as the king who brought this planet under one rule."

"You want me to help you conquer my people and overthrow the House of Draig monarchy?" Mede couldn't believe this man's nerve and had to question his sanity. She let a talon stretch from her fingertip as she worked on snagging the material binding her wrist. The ties held her at an awkward angle and made cutting difficult.

"There is always some resistance to change." His claw made the trip back over her breasts. She was well aware of how dangerous her position was. One angry gesture and this man could rip into her chest. "The key is to have the stronger resolve and to be willing to kill whoever gets in your way."

"It's not too late. You can let me go." Mede tried to sound reasonable. She kept her voice soft, trying to remember what exactly she had said or done to draw this man's twisted affection.

"But we're married. We are on Var land and I claimed you as my half mate. It's done. There is no letting you go, wife, you belong to me." He stepped back. His claw left her chest and she inhaled a deep breath of temporary relief. He looked at his hands. "This won't do."

Mede made a small noise as he reached for her skirt. Grabbing the end, he slashed at it with his claws, cutting it into jagged strips before managing to tear off a chunk of silk and lace. He wiped his bloody hands on it before swiping at his tunic in an effort to clean up.

The open air against her exposed legs caused her to look down at what he'd done. Material wrapped one ankle, hooked around the tree and wrapped the other. It kept her legs apart so she couldn't close them. She tried to shift while he was distracted, but the steel rods in the corset's design bound her chest and stomach too tightly. Unlike her human flesh, the hard skin of the dragon couldn't mold to the clothing's shape. Even trying was too painful.

Mede had never been in a situation where she'd had to fight like a woman and not a dragon. "Attor. I need you to untie me."

He turned his gaze sharply to her.

"This is no way to begin a marriage." She tried to smile at him. "Come on. Untie me. Let me walk to my new palace with dignity."

Attor laughed. "Nice try, my lady, but I'm not stupid and you're not that good of an actress. Your anger shows in your burning eyes." He tossed the piece from her torn gown aside and touched her cheek. "But that's all right. I like taming my women. Right now you're frightened because of your innocence."

"Or because you hit me over the head, and tied me to a tree," she answered.

"There's that fire I saw in you the night we met." Attor clapped his hands. "You're not so tough when you're not carrying a blade, are you?"

Mede slowly began to recall more of their first conversation. She remembered thinking this man was handsome, but now she didn't see it. "I remember you said that you have no reason to harm women."

"I also said we weren't at war. At that time, we weren't. Now—"

"So you do want to start a war." Mede felt the ties holding her wrists snag on the bark and began to work her arms while he was distracted.

"That will depend largely on you, wife." Attor studied her and she stopped moving. "You really are worthy of royalty. I wish I could see King Tared's face when he discovers you are married to me and not his son." His expression fell and she wondered at the strangeness of his cloudy gaze. "We will have many sons. You were right when you said being an only child is a burden and our parents were weak for not having—"

"I never said that," Mede denied. "You twist my words."

"As my wife, you will be able to bring the dragons to heel." Attor began to pace.

As he spoke, she worked her arms faster. Suddenly, the binds straining against her ankles loosened. Her knees buckled slightly. How did that happen? She hadn't been trying to free her feet yet.

"They will see their prized dragon lady has chosen me over their prince—" Attor continued.

A thud sounded behind her followed by an, "*Aagh.*"

Attor instantly shifted and faced Mede. She flinched, working her wrists faster. If she was attacked, she couldn't defend herself.

LLYR REMAINED quiet as he crept around to where Mede was tied to a tree. Var liked to leap down from tree limbs and he needed to make sure there were no surprise attacks. Saben was behind her, trying to cut her ties. Though they really could have used it, they hadn't had enough time to get more help.

"*Aagh.*"

Llyr turned his attention forward at the noise. Saben lay on the ground behind Mede, holding his head. While Attor's attention was distracted, Llyr charged. Saben rolled to his feet, swaying a little but ready to fight anything that moved too close to him.

Mede thrashed violently, kicking her feet while trapped by her wrists. Attor must have heard Llyr's approach because he turned. Saben fought his attacker. It looked like the same cat-shifter that had fallen on Saben outside the festival.

Llyr felt Mede's eyes on him, and he would fight anyone who tried to keep her from him. He slashed at the Var prince with his talons. Attor roared. Llyr growled. There was no hesitance as they fought. Attor's hand glanced over the hard armor of Llyr's chest. The sharp tips bit into his flesh like tiny needles dragging along his skin. Llyr swept his arm wide, coming down hard against Attor's neck. When the man stumbled, Llyr swung again to hit him on the other side.

Attor jerked and made a strange noise. Llyr saw the blur of movement between the man's legs. Mede had kicked the Var prince in the balls. Hard.

Llyr drew back his fist and punched. Attor's head snapped back and he stumbled before falling to the ground.

Mede kicked her feet out and screeched as she tried to reach Attor's body from her place tied to the tree. He felt her anger as if it was his own. Saben had the other Var pinned to the ground and was choking him.

"Tell me I can kill him," Saben begged. "I should have killed him the first time. He's like a bad batch of ale that keeps coming back to haunt you."

"No," Mede ordered. "Honor dictates we let them live. That is a house noble. I heard them talking when I was coming in and out of consciousness. This is their prince." Mede kicked her foot one last time, still unable to reach Attor's prone form. "If we kill them we are responsible for war. That is what they want."

Llyr went to her. His heart beat so fast he was sure it would explode. He cupped her face to look at her. "Did they hurt you?"

Mede shook her head in denial. He could tell it was a lie. Dried blood encrusted her temple. Her lips parted and he kissed her. All the passion and worry poured into that moment. He accepted her fully, gave her power over everything he was, and in turn he felt her entering his soul. She loved him. He felt it. The very touch of her sent fire through his blood and staked claim to his heart.

"GET OFF MY WIFE!" Attor yelled.

Mede screamed. Llyr was jerked back as the Var prince surged up from the ground and grabbed the back of his tunic. He went for Llyr's neck with extended claws, about to rip out the man's throat.

Mede screamed again. Without thought, she forced her arms forward. The ties snapped. Heat choked her body. The lava of her dragon's blood seared her insides. She screamed again, unable to control it. This time smoke filtered past her lips. Her back expanded painfully against the corset. She saw Attor staring at her in awe, his arm poised for the death strike. She felt the rip of flesh as the corset strings snapped. Her back jerked upward and she lifted off the ground. Unsure how, her body undulated in the air.

She looked down at Attor and burned with hatred. Llyr was shifted and stared up at her in awe and confusion. A flash of a wing caught her attention along her peripheral vision. She had wings. She flew. Another scream ripped out of her, more animal than human, and her breath became pure fire as it rolled out of her lungs.

Attor dove out of the way. She turned her head, trying not to hit Llyr as the primitive dragon tried to take over. She had one driving need—to protect her family.

The crackling of flames lapped trees. She screeched again, but since she knew what was coming, she was able to shoot the fire into the sky. Llyr scrambled to his feet and lifted his taloned hands. He spoke, but she didn't understand his words.

She somehow managed to land. Not because she had the skill to control her new body, but because the dragon instinctively wanted to put Llyr behind her. She watched Attor run from them.

She felt a hand on her ass and turned. Somehow, her butt didn't seem to come with her. Instead Llyr held her tail under his arm to keep it from swinging. He again shouted up at her, holding out his hand. Her eyes focused on the crystal glowing in his palm. Her long neck jerked to again make sure Attor was gone. Fire burned and she snorted smoke from her nose to put it out.

Slowly, her form began to retract in on itself, becoming smaller. The shift hurt, not so much the physical resetting of her bones but rather the willpower it took to reign in the beast. Her body dropped. The tattered remnants of her gown hung on her frame, clinging to one shoulder but not hiding her nakedness beneath. Llyr hurried and pulled off his tunic shirt to slip it over her head. She smelled charred silk.

She breathed heavily, shaking and cold. "Llyr? Are you burned?"

He lifted his arms and first one bare leg, then the other. She'd scorched his pants so they hung about his waist like a silken loincloth, but his skin was unharmed.

"It actually kind of tickled," Llyr said. The

crystal glow radiated over his beautiful face as he held the stone toward her. "I told you, my lady, you are my fate."

"How did you get that?" She rushed to him, so very glad she didn't injure him. The stone wasn't his broken one, but it did glow brighter when she came near him.

"It's mine. The gods gave it back to me. I wasn't lying when I said you make my crystal glow. I'm sorry I tricked you by wearing my servant's stone. I wanted you to get to know me first. I really did break my arm trying to trick-ride ceffyls, but not my stone. I'm sorry I didn't tell you the truth from the beginning. I promise I'll explain everything once we're to safety."

"I knew it," Saben yelled. He jumped up and down excitedly while covering his mouth. Between his fingers, he said, "You *can* fly!"

"Why didn't you shift and free yourself sooner?" Llyr asked, trying to ignore Saben.

"I tried. I couldn't." She still shivered with cold. The fire had taken her body heat with it. "My mother put me in that stupid corset again. It was too constrictive." She wrapped her arms around Llyr and hugged him tightly, burying her head in his chest. "I was so scared you wouldn't find me. That lunatic tried to say I was his half mate."

"He claimed you?" Saben asked, gasping. He

lifted his hand and let a talon grow on the end. "You have to let me go after him and kill him. I will do it. Your hands will be clean. She cannot be married to two—"

Mede picked up the bloody piece of material Attor had shredded from her gown. She lifted the material and held it over to Llyr's eyes to symbolize the mask he had been wearing at the ceremony. But since it was dirty, she didn't touch him with it. "I choose you, Prince Llyr, as my husband." She pulled it away and dropped the material on the ground.

"Huh." Saben looked at them both and then gave a small shrug. "Looked binding and official to me."

The ceremony was hardly tradition, but she didn't care. "You're mine, Llyr. And I'm yours."

"Uh, you two might want to hurry things along." Saben walked over to where the noble had begun to stir. He leaned over and punched the Var hard to knock him back out. "Someone is bound to notice if the dragon prince doesn't show up tomorrow morning to announce his marriage. I don't know how many more of these damned cats are out roaming tonight, but the fire spouts are bound to have drawn some notice."

"He's right," Llyr said.

"Kiss me, Llyr. Now," she demanded. "You don't want to upset a dragon female."

Llyr obliged. She moaned into his mouth, letting his tongue roll past her lips. His body heat warmed her chilled skin. She heard his whispering in her mind, *I love you, Mede, I want you.*

Forever, she answered.

"Seriously, we have to go now," Saben prodded.

"Can you run?" Llyr asked.

"Just try to catch me." Mede shifted into her normal dragon form and took off into the forest. The tattered pieces of her dress dangled around her legs as she ran. Llyr and Saben gave chase.

"Mede," Saben yelled in excitement as they darted through the woods. "You looked just like the dragon tapestries. You had wings and a tail. And you spit fire! Oh, do me next? Set me on fire. Please, Mede. I want scorched clothes, too. Can you shift into the full dragon again?"

Mede ran faster.

"Hey, can you at least fly us home? That might be quicker." Saben tried to keep up.

"Sorry, Saben," Mede answered, "there's only one dragon who lights my fire."

CHAPTER 17

Mede did not want to wait to seal their fate. When they made it back to the encampment the sun was just starting to lighten the morning. It was early yet and many of the wedding couples still slept. However, the festival raged on and the drunken crowd was only too willing to stare after the tattered trio as they emerged from the forest. Llyr wore his silken loincloth and nothing else. He held the crystal stone minus the leather strap that had withered to ash. Mede had a bracelet and partial veil tied to one wrist, a scorched male tunic that barely had enough material to hang over her breasts, and a very revealing skirt of cat-shredded strips. Saben was just missing his shirt. He'd taken it off and rubbed dirt on his skin so he'd look as battle-worn as the bridal couple.

Queen Lorna dozed in her chair and the king talked with one of the elders. At Llyr's approach, he instantly stood in worry. The crowd quieted. The strums of the *gittern* tripped to a stop. The queen's head came up at the silence. She blinked heavily.

"Queen Lorna. King Tared. May I present Lady Medellyn, my true wife?" Confused cheering erupted at the sound. The queen looked over their attire with a stricken expression. The king started to cross over to his son, only to stop when Llyr lifted his crystal.

"I believe you have some experience with this," he said, lifting it to Mede. "Shall I find a rock from the forest for you?"

Mede arched a brow. "How do you know that's how I destroyed my...?"

"I saw you that day running in the forest and I followed you," Llyr admitted. "You were so angry and I wanted to help. When you stopped, I didn't think you wanted company, so I watched you just to make sure you were fine. My crystal didn't glow as I was too young, but I knew I had to wait for you. I felt you were going to be my bride."

Mede gave a soft laugh. "You and every other boy I came across."

"I think this proves me right." Llyr handed her his glowing crystal.

She took it, dropped it on the ground and stomped on it. A small sensation worked over her like a shiver. Mede grinned, so very happy. The pain of her long night became more forceful now that the crystal's glow wasn't luring her to it like a euphoric painkiller.

"Welcome to the family, Lady Medellyn. I hope you will enjoy your new home," the Queen stated loudly so the crowd could hear her blessing. Then she hurried over to her husband's side, closer to the couple.

"Thank you," Mede acknowledged. "I'm sorry I didn't get a chance to accept your invitation to the palace sooner. I did not mean to ignore them all."

"All?" The queen looked confused. "I don't understand. Have I missed something?"

"Oh, yeah," Llyr said with a guilty look. "I might have written those invitations." He gave Mede a sheepish smile. "I really, *really* wanted to meet you. But that's it. That's all I wasn't fully honest about. I promise no more deceptions."

"What happened tonight? Why is there blood on your clothing?" King Tared eyed his son and new daughter with worry.

Llyr motioned to Saben to come onto the platform and the man jumped up. "He'll explain everything. As for me, I'm taking my wife to the bridal tent for some much needed sleep."

Mede smiled as he hooked her arm and led her away. Drunken blessings and well wishes came from those they passed. As Llyr lifted the tent's flap, Mede paused and said, "You really don't think I'm going to let you sleep now that you're my husband?"

"Beautiful wife, I am yours to command. Do with me what you will." Llyr leaned to kiss her.

"Oh, I intend to, my prince." Mede grabbed him by his shirt and tugged him into the tent behind her. "Believe me, I intend to."

ATTOR WALKED the length of the palace hall to his bedchamber. Nothing could lighten the sourness of his mood. He'd lost Mede. He'd lost his only chance at happiness and love. The obsession he felt for her would not lessen, so instead it turned to hatred, and focused on revenge. He would not kill her. No, that would be too easy, but he would take everything she loved. "I will bide my time, Lady Medellyn, and even if it takes a hundred years, I will destroy everything you love. Have your sons with Prince Llyr. Watch them grow. And when they try to start their families you will see your lines crumble. You will watch your sons lose what you have taken from me—their mates."

"There you are." Myrddin appeared, looking as battered as Attor. "Did you hear the news? Your father was found dead this evening. Apparently he's been rotting in his bedchamber for a few days. The maids thought he was sleeping off one of his drunken stupors and did not want to risk waking him. When the cooks noticed no meals were being requested, one guard ventured in and found him."

Attor stiffened, remembering his father's still body under his hands. He should have known this moment would come, but it hadn't and so he'd tried to push the reality of his deeds from his mind.

"You're the new king," Myrddin exclaimed. "And after tonight, you have to agree. War can finally begin."

A small fear that his actions were known filled him and he lashed out. "What did you do to my father?" Attor shouted at the old house noble.

"Nothing," Myrddin swore in surprise. "I did nothing. He died in his sleep."

"I don't believe you. You talked of killing him when we were in the forest." Attor pointed accusingly at him. "Tell me now. Do they suspect foul play?"

"I swear he died a natural death, my king. I did not have the old king killed. You must believe me." Myrddin fell to his knees. "I would not betray you, my king."

The title was hardly official since there had been no coronation, but it did flatter Attor's pride, so he did not correct it.

Attor pretended to consider the noble's answer. Finally, he slowly nodded. "I believe you. Now stand and go. I want sleep."

"Do you want me to send a woman to ease you?" Myrddin rose to his feet.

Attor thought of his swollen balls where Mede had kicked him. "No. If I wanted a woman I would have told you to bring me one. Go and make sure I'm not disturbed. I'm going to grieve the sudden shock of my father's passing."

"Yes, my king," Myrddin backed out of the room.

MEDE EYED the new design for a wedding dress with a look of both horror and amusement. Apparently, her debut as the new princess had caused quite a stir—especially when Saben's tale of her bravery in the face of a Var kidnapping somehow made it over the countryside. Of course, no one believed him when he said she could fly. Mede could hardly believe that part herself. All she could reason was that her love for Llyr had surged forth to protect him. She remembered the dragon's feeling of family and protection. She guessed if Llyr's life ever was in danger again, the dragon would show herself. Until then, Mede's shifting had resumed to normal.

"Apparently," Queen Lorna said with an amused smile as she lowered the paper, "the grooms think this new outfit will be lucky and bless their marriages with strong women like the new princess."

They were in the royal office where the family often gathered to socialize away from the eyes of servants. Being married to a prince was hard to get used to, but there were perks—like an incredibly devoted husband she couldn't keep her hands off of.

"What about the grooms? If the brides have to be mostly naked, don't you think the men should be punished as well?" Mede liked her new mother-by-marriage very much. She'd been very welcoming in the many months since her marriage to Llyr.

"I was thinking loincloths," Queen Lorna whispered. "Tiny bits of fur and nothing else."

Mede laughed, gasping as she nodded. "Yes, please. Saben will be thrilled, though I'm not sure anyone else will be. Only you had better not mention it to my mother when she comes to visit tomorrow. The last time I spoke to her, she had ideas for changes she wanted me to implement now that I have power. She said something about starting a movement to end liquor consumption, fighting in front of women, and the Order of the Dead Dragons."

"If anyone can do it, your mother can. That woman is amazing. The way she gets these dragons to do whatever she wants without raising her voice." The queen sighed in admiration. "That's a talent."

"It's the sugared biscuits," Mede said. "Apparently, men will do almost anything for sweet foods."

"I'll remember that the next time the king tries to convince me to go camping in the forest." The queen stood. "The men should be done meeting with the new commander soon. I'm anxious to hear what they found out. King Attor has been too quiet this last year. I'd like to think that he feels sorry for his misguided attempts at marriage, but I'm afraid this may be the quiet before the storm."

Mede watched as the queen left her alone in the office. She closed her eyes, trying to beckon Llyr to her side. Within moments, he was running through the door to her.

"You called, my princess?" He always had a smile for her.

"I did, my prince. Any news from the commander?" Mede didn't bother to stand as she reached her hand up to him.

"Still quiet. No signs of Var movement in the forest." Llyr took her hand and kissed it before leaning over the arm of the chair to kiss her properly. "I know you are worried he might try to strike at this next Breeding Festival, but there is no evidence he's planning an attack. We've been vigilant all year. The warriors are better trained than they were last year. Soldiers have been posted along the borderland and there will be a heavy presence around the festival grounds. I've even asked that Galaxy Brides does a scan for heat signatures in the forest before they land. It will be safe."

"You know, I was thinking, we never got to experience our night in the bridal tent. Don't get me wrong, I enjoyed making very tired love to you the next morning before passing out for twelve hours, but I think I want the full experience."

Llyr began to nod but suddenly pulled back. "Wait, no. You do remember that couples aren't supposed to have sex the night before the crystal is broken? They can talk and play, but they can't find release."

"What? Are you scared you're not up to it?" she challenged.

Llyr laughed. "Oh, you're on, my beautiful princess. We'll see who begs who first."

Mede moaned softly into his mouth. Her body tingled with longing. A year had done nothing to cool her desires for him. "Good thing that's still a few weeks away."

"What do you mean?" He stroked her hair back from her face.

She leaned to whisper hotly into his ear, "Carry me to our room and you'll find out."

Llyr swept her up into his arms before she could finish the sentence. He ran through the palace halls, not caring if the servants saw them.

"I love you, forever, lady wife," he said as he pushed through the thick door to their private wing.

"Yes," Mede whispered. "I love you, forever."

The End

THE SERIES CONTINUES...

**Want to see how King Attor's sons turn out,
despite their father's teachings?
Next book in the series installments:**

Lords of the Var®: The Savage King

**Was this your first Dragon Lords?
Go back to the beginning!**

Dragon Lords 1: Barbarian Prince

**Read all the Dragon Lords and Var books?
Yay, you, keep going!**

Space Lords 1: (His) Frost Maiden

THE SAVAGE KING
BY MICHELLE M. PILLOW

The Series Continues...

Curious to see the Var side of things?

Lords of the Var® Book One
A Qurilixen World Novel
Bestselling Cat-shifter Romance Series

CAT-SHIFTING King Kirill knows he must do his
duty by his people. When his father unexpectedly
dies, it's his destiny to take the throne and all of the
responsibility that entails. What he hadn't prepared
for is the troublesome prisoner that's now his to
deal with.

Undercover Agent Ulyssa is no man's captive.
Trapped in a primitive forest awaiting pickup, she's

going to make the best out of a bad situation… which doesn't include falling for the seductions of a king.

About *Lords of the Var*® (Books 1-5)

YOU MET THEIR FATHER, King Attor, in Dragon Lords Books 1-4, now meet the Var Princes!

The cat-shifter princes were raised to not believe in love, especially love for one woman, and they will do everything in their power to live up to their father's expectations. Oh, how the mighty will fall.

The Savage King Excerpt

KIRILL WATCHED the door to his bedroom open. He'd been sitting in the dark, trying to relieve the stress headache that had built behind his eyes for the last week. The pain started at the base of his skull and radiated up to his temples until he could hardly see straight.

A heavy responsibility had been thrust on his shoulders, a responsibility he really hadn't prepared himself for, the welfare of the Var people. King Attor had not left him in a good position. He'd rallied the people to the brink of war, convinced them that the Draig were their enemy, and even went so far as to attack the Draig royal family.

Kirill wanted to see peace in the land. However, he knew the facts didn't bode well for it. The Draig had a long list of grievances against King Attor and the Var kingdom.

Before his death, the king had ordered an attack on the four Draig princes, all of which ended horribly for the Var. The worst was when Prince Yusef was stabbed in the back, a most cowardly embarrassment for the Var guard who did it. If he hadn't been executed in the Draig prisons, he would've been ostracized from the Var community. Luckily, Prince Yusef survived or they'd already be at battle.

Attor had also arranged for the kidnapping of Yusef's new bride. The Draig Princess Olena had been rescued, or that too would've led to war. The old king had even tried to poison Princess Morrigan, the future Draig queen, on two separate occasions. She too lived. And those were only a few of the offenses Kirill knew about in the few weeks before King Attor's death. He could just imagine what he didn't know.

Kirill sighed, feeling very tired. He'd known

since birth that the day would come when he'd be expected to step up and lead the Var as their new king. He just hadn't expected it to be for another hundred or so years. His father had been a hard man, whom he'd foolishly believed was invincible.

"Here kitty, kitty, kitty." His lovely houseguest's whisper drew his complete attention from his heavy thoughts.

Ulyssa bent over like she expected him to answer to the insulting call. He dropped his fingers from his temple into his lap, and a quizzical smile came to his lips. As he watched her, he wasn't sure if he was angered or amused by her words.

"Are you in here, you little furball?" she said, a little louder.

She wore his clothes. Never had the outfit looked sexier. His jaw tightened in masculine interest, as he unabashedly looked her over. All too well did he remember the softness of her body against his and the gentle, offering pleasure of her sweet lips. She'd made soft whimpering noises when he'd touched her, yielding, purring sounds in the back of her throat. Even with the aid of nef, he was surprised by how easily and confidently she melted into him. The Var were wild, passionate people and were drawn to the same qualities in others. He suspected she'd be an untamed lover.

Too bad she'd belonged to his father first. In his

mind, that made her completely untouchable though none would dare question his claim if he were to take her to his bed. Technically, by Var law, she belonged to him until he chose to release her. For an insane moment, he thought about keeping her as a lover. He knew he wouldn't, but the thought was entertaining.

Kirill's grin deepened. Ulyssa strode across his home to the bathroom door with an irritated scowl. It was obvious she didn't see him in the darkened corner, watching her. He detected her engaging smell from across the room, the smell of a woman's desire. It stirred his blood, making his limbs heavy with arousal. And, for the first time since his father's death, his headache relieved itself.

"Hum, maybe I'm looking too high. I'm sure there has to be a little cat door here somewhere. Come here, little kitty. Where are you hiding?"

His slight smile fell at her words. It was easy to detect her mocking tone.

"Where's your little kitty door, huh?" Ulyssa whispered to herself, her blue gaze searching around in the dark.

Kirill grimaced in further displeasure. He watched her open the door to his weapons cabinet. Her eyes rounded, and he thought she might take one. She didn't. Instead, she nodded in appreciation before closing the door and continuing her search for an exit.

She stopped at a narrow window by his kitchen doorway. Her neck craned to the side, as she tried to see out over the distance. Kirill knew she looked at the forest. From under her breath, he heard her vehement whisper, "Where exactly did you little fur balls bring me? Ugh, I need to get out of this flea trap, even if I have to fight every one of you cowardly felines to do it. I've fought species twice as big and three times as frightening. A couple of little kitty cats don't scare me."

If this insolent woman wanted to play tough, oh, he'd play. Curling gracefully forward, Kirill shifted before his hands even touched the ground. He let one thick paw land silently on the floor, followed by a second. Short black fur rippled over his tanned flesh, blending him into the shadows. His clothes fell from his body, and he lowered his head as he crept forward. A low sound of warning started in the back of his throat. He was livid.

To find out more about Michelle's books visit www.MichellePillow.com

New York Times & _USA TODAY_
Bestselling Author

Michelle loves to travel and try new things, whether it's a paranormal investigation of an old Vaudeville Theatre or climbing Mayan temples in Belize. She believes life is an adventure fueled by copious amounts of coffee.

Newly relocated to the American South. Michelle is involved in various film and documentary projects with her talented director husband. She is mom to a fantastic artist. And she's managed by a dog and cat who make sure she's meeting her deadlines.

For the most part she can be found wearing pajama pants and working in her office. There may or may not be dancing. It's all part of the creative process.

Come say hello! Michelle loves talking with readers on social media!

www.MichellePillow.com

facebook.com/AuthorMichellePillow

twitter.com/michellepillow

instagram.com/michellempillow

bookbub.com/authors/michelle-m-pillow

goodreads.com/Michelle_Pillow

amazon.com/author/michellepillow

youtube.com/michellepillow

pinterest.com/michellepillow

COMPLIMENTARY EXCERPTS

HIS FROST MAIDEN

BY MICHELLE M. PILLOW

Read all the Dragon Lords and Var books?
Yay, you, keep going!

A Qurilixen World Novel
Space Lords Book One

Bestselling Futuristic Romance Series

Empath and space pirate, Evan Cormier is
obsessed with decoding an ominous premonition
about his future. When a fellow crewman angered a
spirit, the vengeful Zhang An took her wrath out
on everyone in the vicinity. Evan just happened to
be one of them. He's now facing a future in which
he'll be forever alone.

Lady Josselyn of the House of Craven has been

betrayed. With her home world on a Florencian moon under attack and her family dead, she finds herself at the mercy of the one who deceived them. There is only one thing left to do—die with honor. But before she can join her family in the afterlife, she must first avenge all that she held dear. Falling in love with a pirate was never in the plan. Evan and his thieving crewmates might have delayed her fate, but they can't stop destiny.

Frost Maiden Excerpt

Craven Estates, Earth Settlement, Florencia's Fifth Moon

"Lift her," the General ordered, his shiny boots walking away from her, taking her reflection with it.

Two men hauled her to her feet, holding her up by her arms. Josselyn suppressed a cry as they jerked her dislocated shoulder. She couldn't see their faces, didn't need to. Her body hurt so badly she couldn't tell where the pain was coming from anymore.

The one who'd betrayed them stood before her. General Jack Stephans. He'd deceived her family and the fifth moon settlement. He'd traded them in for money and power. Josselyn lifted her gaze briefly to the hard depths of the steel green eyes before her. She wanted to kick, to give one last good blow, to go down fighting, but she couldn't raise her limbs.

"Poor little Josselyn, so heartbreaking," the General grabbed her chin and swiped beneath her eye. He looked young, was in fact very young for his position, only a few years older than her six and twenty. And yet they all knew so much more of fighting than anyone their age should, than anyone ever should.

"We gave you a home," she whispered. "How could you do this? How could you join them?"

"You gave me a place in your stables," he spat, his grip tightening on her chin, bruisingly so. "Not a place at your table. Not a place by your side. Not equal. They gave me a rank, a title. They give me respect. They give me a place in this world."

"Jack," she said, her voice softening for the orphan boy they'd found over twenty years ago. If she begged him, maybe fate could be turned around; maybe this day could be erased. Fate had spit them out in a whirlwind of chance and deceit. Maybe all that had happened wasn't his fault. Maybe it wasn't hers. None of it mattered. None of it changed the fact that he had taken everything she held dear, everyone, and now he was robbing her of her family home. Her tone hardened and she closed her eyes. "General."

"Look at me, Josselyn," he said. His tone caught even as his grip on her face tightened until his fingers pressed the inside of her cheeks against her teeth. "You're so cold. Even now, your face is composed. Is one, lonely tear all the passion you can muster?"

"I am Lady Josselyn of the House of Craven." Her eyes opened slowly, focusing on the shiny white of his uniform. It gleamed with the orange glow coming from the fireplace. The material looked odd in the drabber earth tones many on the fifth moon wore. Theirs was a world based on Medieval Earth. Each moon in the Florencian system was different, each settlement patterned off a singular time in the human past, times that history had almost forgotten. But the principals of the ancestors who'd established the colonies no longer applied. Times were different now. What had started as preservation of history had turned into reality, into laws and a way of life they all believed in as generation after generation was raised into the worlds of the Florencian moons.

The General shook her by the face until finally she forced her eyes to meet his. He looked angry, hurt, wildly hopeful. "I can save you. I can say you had nothing to do with the treachery of your family. No one wants to kill a woman of noble blood. The line of Craven doesn't have to die. I will take your name; the name denied me by your father."

Was he serious? She knew he'd asked her father for her hand in marriage. In fact, she'd dismissed the proposal with the full knowledge he only asked because he wanted power. Did he think she could love him now? Want him? Take him into her bed?

He must have read the answer on her face because his own expression hardened. She knew Jack. He wouldn't ask again.

"I suppose not," he said, almost sad. "Even if you agreed, I could never trust you not to take a blade to my back. Not after today." He sighed heavily. "Not after this."

"Ago," she whispered, even her voice beginning to fail in its strength, "pugna quod int-"

"Quiet your tongue! This house is mine. Mine." He let go of her chin and her head drooped. "And you can die knowing that I have taken more than what you all refused to give me in life."

"A place at our table," Josselyn said, her tone softer still, the will to live leaving her. Her heart called out to her ancestors, to her dead family, begging them to come and get her.

"My table," he answered, stepping away. The General lifted a gun, pointing it at her head. She heard the telltale click of metal on metal. The weapon was not one found on the fifth moon. They fought with swords and axes, like the old medieval ways. Though technology was available, not using it was a point of honor. He must have brought the weapon from another moon. Perhaps the Victorians? The Elizabethans? It appeared to be too old to be from much later in time.

"Do it, Jack." She didn't look at him as she waited for the final discharge of the gun, the loud bang before the end. When it didn't come, she repeated, the words a mere mouthing of her lips, "Do it."

"Speed you to a quick end, Josselyn Craven," Jack whispered. "You all brought this on yourselves."

**To find out more about Michelle's books
visit www.MichellePillow.com**

DETERMINED PRINCE

CAPTURED BY A DRAGON-SHIFTER

by Michelle M. Pillow
A Modern Day Dragon Lords Story
A Qurilixen World Novel

Dragon-shifter Prince Kyran has studied the Earth people and is ready to assimilate. Female shifters are all but going extinct on his planet of Qurilixen, and his people are desperate for mates—so much so they're taking matters into their own hands. What better place to capture a woman than Earth? After all, dragon-shifters had come from there centuries ago. Surely a human female would be honored to be selected by one as fine and fierce as himself?

While on Earth, Kyran stumbles upon the most beautiful woman he's ever imagined, singing something the natives call rock 'n' roll. His blood simmers and he knows Eve is the one for him. But taming this feisty female is going to take much more than his training prepared him for.

To find out more about Michelle's books visit www.MichellePillow.com

HIS EARTH MAIDEN

Space Lords Series

Former elite Federation soldier, now turned space pirate, Jackson Burke has done his best to turn his life around—for the better. He isn't prepared when fate leaves a woman's safety totally in his hands. Since heroes don't leave a damsel in distress—and despite being outlaw pirates, the crew considers themselves the good guys—Jackson assumes responsibility for the beauty. It's enough that his ship is held together by rust and sheer will, now he's got to keep this good guy thing straight and not give into the urges the sassy female brings out in him. Raisa is everything a man could want and for some reason she seems to like him, rough edges and all, but he's on the Federation's wanted list and they aren't known to back down.

Space Lords Series
His Frost Maiden
His Fire Maiden
His Metal Maiden
His Earth Maiden
His Woodland Maiden

CHAPTER ONE EXCERPT

Torgan Black Market
  City of Madaga, Planet of Torgan
  There were defining moments in his life when Jackson Burke had known things would never be the same. The day he had been compelled as a young boy living in an orphanage to join the Federation Military—more from a longing for adventure than a sense of galactic duty. The day he was promoted into a secret program to create super soldiers, where he was tested on, trained, and held to the highest of standards. The day he met Captain Jarek and signed on to sail the high skies as a security officer on a pirate ship instead of staying with the Federation,

much to the military's disappointment. The day their pilot, Rick, had insulted a vengeful spirit who put a love curse on the heads of five of the crewmen.

And today, the day he decided it was a good day to die.

Death had come calling for him more times than he could count. By all rights, he should have been blown up, or incinerated, or sucked into deep space, or crash landed on some remote planet. Actually, in all those cases, he probably could have blamed Rick. Half the time, the crew couldn't decide if they wanted to save their pilot from trouble or leave his stupid ass behind.

Rick was the reason they were currently stranded on Torgan with a broken ship they couldn't afford to fix.

Bound Virgin wasn't technically their ship. It belonged to Princess Samantha of the Var—the former captain who had kidnapped a shifter prince named Falke and ultimately married him. She wouldn't be happy that her ship was out of commission. Jackson had been sailing the high skies with Falke's brother Jarek at the time of the kidnapping. When Jarek married and settled down, his crew and Samantha's crew had merged. Captain Lochlann and Jackson now flew with Rick, brothers Lucien and Viktor, and Dev. Lochlann's wife,

Alexis, and Dev's wife, Violette, also traveled with them.

Jackson guessed none of that history mattered anymore, seeing as he faced the end. Because there was no way in all the blasted space novas he was going back into the Federation Military. There had been a time when he believed in greater causes, but he'd been young and impressionable. At that age, all young men had wanted to believe they were part of a solution. But the Federation wasn't purely good, and their missions were not against evil. Jackson had seen too much corruption in his travels. Yes, the military had its place. The men who served were some of the best he'd ever known. But Jackson felt he'd done his duty. He wasn't going back.

Three young soldiers surrounded him, as if to block him from escape. They had the eager expressions of cadets on their first mission. Jackson could evade them and run, but that would mean putting a target on his back. The inability of the Federation to find him is the only thing that kept them from forcing him back into service. He knew how this would go. The Federation didn't ask. They commanded.

"Soldier J-67114, upon contact, we have orders to detain—"

Jackson lifted his eyes from the ground to look

at the young recruit talking to him. That one expression was enough to cut off the man's words. The black uniform was standard issue, without any distinctions of rank or battle. The man looked at his handheld device and swallowed nervously. Jackson crossed his arms over his chest and widened his stance.

The soldier tried again. "We have orders to inform you that you are to be detained for—"

"No," Jackson interrupted.

"What did you say?" The soldier looked confused.

"No," Jackson repeated.

"What do you mean, no?" He looked to his buddies for help.

"The Federation really let their standards slip when they enlisted you, didn't they? No is a word derived from the Old Star language that means you better get out of my way or I'll launch you into deep space."

The soldier glanced up as if Jackson would actually throw him through the glass and metal ceiling of the trading center. It wasn't unusual to run into Federation soldiers on the planet of Torgan, but Jackson tended to avoid them when he could. It was an unspoken understanding that, unless there was a serious threat, the military left the traders who came to the black-market planet alone. Apparently, this was one overly eager recruit who hadn't been given the memo.

The Torgan marketplace kept up the appearance of being a legitimate trading center and made enough space credits to slip money into the hands of all the right officials. Ships from around the galaxies landed on the grayish-brown orb.

From the sky, the planet didn't look like much—a desert of dust and sand which was ill-suited to anything but storing space trash, and whose three rings wrapping the planet's sky were the only hint of natural beauty in the desolate landscape. Despite this, the planet thrived because underneath the adobe-style businesses surrounding the large trading complex, lay a darker purpose. If it was fenced, illegal, tawdry, or sought after, someone on Torgan would have it for sale. If there was a price to be had or a deal to be made, someone would make it and very few questions would be asked. Want someone killed? Ask around the center bar. Need stolen medical supplies? Ask around the docks. Need—

"You're J-67114," the soldier insisted.

Jackson lied. "No."

"But your scan—" The soldier held up his device as if that was infallible evidence.

Jackson grabbed the handheld and threw it

against a wall. "Looks broken. You should ask for a new one."

"That's Federation property. By order of the… the…" The soldier tried to pull his blaster from his waist.

"Run," Jackson ordered under his breath. "Or I'll throw you next. You have no idea what you're getting yourself into."

Jackson felt a blaster press to the small of his back.

He hadn't forgotten the other two. He had just hoped they'd be smart enough to back away from the situation.

He glanced over the docking platform. Ships were lined up in tight formation along the concrete area. No one landed or took off without permission, so even if their ship wasn't broken, he wouldn't be making a fast escape.

"Why don't you go see if the Galaxy Playmates show is about to start?" Jackson suggested. He paused as a group of slender Klennup males walked by in shiny gold suits. When they were out of earshot, he continued, "Forget you saw me. Tell them your hand-held was broken in a bar fight. They'll believe it. Bar fights happen about every three minutes—"

"You don't look too tough with a blaster in your back," the soldier behind him jeered.

Jackson caught Rick leaning against a wall near the main complex's entrance. The man was as human as they came, with short brown hair, brown eyes, and the same irritatingly amused expression regardless of the situation. The pilot grinned and made no move to help him. Someone caught Rick's attention, and he motioned them forward.

Dev appeared in the entryway. People were usually terrified of his red skin and black eyes. If that didn't scare a person, then his large size would.

Instead of helping, Dev crossed his arms and nodded once, as if ready for a show. Unless Jackson called out to him, he would not join the fight.

"Last chance to walk away—" Jackson tried to offer.

His words were cut off as a sharp blow hit the back of his head.

Instinct and training kicked in. He swung around, ducking as he maneuvered his elbow into the soldier's stomach. The blaster went flying, but he didn't hear it land against the hard floor. He punched back, making contact with the man's jaw to send him stumbling.

Every fighting move the Federation had taught these men, Jackson had mastered long ago. Every dirty fighting trick they might have, Jackson had probably faced in his years sailing the high skies. It was over before it had started. As the man with the blaster fell, Jackson punched the second man and swept his leg into the knees of the third.

A slow clap sounded as the last man fell. Jackson straightened and frowned. He hadn't wanted this mess. It was random bad luck that these three had been out scanning for trouble.

Rick clapped, still grinning. Dev held the blaster he'd caught when the first soldier fell.

"Blasted space cadets," Jackson swore.

A large, hairy alien walked past, paused to look at the three fallen men and laughed. The sound rumbled from his chest in low, hard beats. He didn't stop to help. At least that was one thing in Jackson's favor. Not too many Torgan visitors would be bothered by what had happened.

Dev picked up the handheld Jackson had smashed against the wall. He thrust it at Jackson. "Get on the ship and don't come off. I'll send Viktor to see what he can salvage from the data."

"We need space credits," Jackson denied. "I'm supposed to be at the Frendle's Chips table."

Gambling was just one of the ways they were able to earn. Lochlann was trying to sell whatever they didn't need. Rick and Lucien were trying to sell what they'd, um, found abandoned on remote planets. Those items required a special buyer. Viktor sold his services as a mechanic doing repairs on the dock. Though no one told the women, Dev's role was to keep an eye on them and make sure they didn't fall into trouble. Alexis and Violette were capable, but their husbands worried. Jackson found it amusing. He felt sorry for any man who tried to cross those two females.

"Go," Dev ordered.

Jackson could have refused. He was the ship's security officer. But, out of all the crewmen, he'd spent the most time with Dev. They'd fought side by side for hours in the virtual reality training room. He had learned to trust his friend's judgment.

Jackson carried the handheld toward the ship. Seeing the hunk of metal resting useless in its space, he frowned. There was nothing worse for a sailor than being landlocked. The fun of visiting planets and fuel docks was knowing they could always take off the second things became too rough.

It would be a shame if they had to scrap their ship as junk metal. Though it wasn't much to look at, when it was running it was a fine vessel. Previous owners had installed medical units in all the rooms. He wasn't one hundred percent sure of the history—the ship's records were as fake as Rick's pretend girlfriends—but he deduced the ship had belonged to Kintok sex traders at one point.

Secret compartments and manacles over beds kind of gave it away.

The ship scanner recognized him and opened as he neared the bottom hatch. He jumped up and pulled himself in through the small opening before the ladder could make its way down. He hit a button, closing himself inside.

The lights running along the walls flickered at half power, but he could find his way around in the dark. An electrical system malfunction had ignited a confined gas pocket, which then destroyed vital parts of the propulsion system. Without it, the ship would chug slowly through the deep black, most likely running out of life support before reaching the next planet. They were lucky to be alive.

Jackson could handle the dark, but it was the silence that bothered him. With the engines off, there was no vibration against his feet. The lights flickered, giving a small buzz as they tried to light his way as sensors detected his presence. He stepped a little louder than normal just to hear the *thud* of his feet on the metal. There were no voices in the cockpit or in the dining hall. There was no music from old transmission waves they'd captured.

He went to the cockpit and sat in the pilot's chair. The Federation device wouldn't turn on, so he set it aside. He doubted it would tell them why the military wanted him back, but maybe Viktor could erase it, break it down and sell off the parts.

Unwilling to sit in the dim light in silence, Jackson pulled up the security feed to watch outside the ship. The lights in the corridor behind him flickered as power was diverted to the screens. He settled back into the pilot's chair and kicked up his feet. A few aliens walked by, the only entertainment as they briefly sauntered past to leave him staring at an empty concrete walkway.

To find out more about Michelle's books visit www.MichellePillow.com

www.ingramcontent.com/pod-product-compliance
Lightning Source LLC
Chambersburg PA
CBHW031955130726
47904CB00013B/1615